MORE PRAISE FOR *COBALT BLUE*

"One of the most shocking and brilliantly worded stories of love. . . . The story will stick with you, and long after you read it, the novel will play on your mind, forcing you to revisit it from time to time."
—Andre Borges, "34 Books by Indian Authors That Everyone Should Read," *Buzzfeed*

"This is a slim, sensual book written in a direct conversational style that makes for very pleasurable reading. I'm passionate about regional Indian fiction, and this unusual and important narrative, so controversial when it was first published many years ago, and the equal of which you won't find in Indian English, is one reason why."
—Sonia Faleiro, *Beautiful Thing: Inside the Secret World of Bombay's Dance Bars*

"*Cobalt Blue* is the kind of book that Franz Kafka called the 'axe for the frozen sea within us' . . . this novel, with its complex narrative design and daring imagination, easily surpasses most English-language fiction that has appeared in India so far this year."

—Livemint

"*Cobalt Blue* reads like a love song. . . . Kundalkar's writing is masterful in its play of voice, capturing through his characters the claustrophobia of a small town, their longing to escape a middle class existence, and how love, and being in love, has the ability to transform every small detail from the mundane to the magnificent."

—Scroll.in

"In the sense of navigating the inner world of an adolescent in the first person, *Cobalt Blue* may be considered a high-quality 'coming-of-age' novel. It also explores the discovery, resulting confusion, and bravado of homosexuality in a hostile environment. . . . This book could be read in one sitting, over the course of one enjoyable day. However, the impact of its characters and what we learn from them would last quite a while longer."

—The Hindu

Cobalt
Blue

A Novel

Sachin Kundalkar

translated from the Marathi
by Jerry Pinto

THE NEW PRESS

NEW YORK
LONDON

First published as *Cobalt Blue* by Mouj Prakashan, 2006
Published in India by Hamish Hamilton, a division of Penguin
    Books India, New Delhi, 2013
Published in the United States by The New Press, New York, 2016
Distributed by Perseus Distribution

LIBRARY OF CONGRESS CATALOGING-IN-PUBLICATION DATA

Names: Kurnrdalakara, Sacina. | Pinto, Jerry, translator.
Title: Cobalt blue : a novel / Sachin Kundalkar ; translated from
    the Marathi by Jerry Pinto.
Other titles: Kobealrta bleu. English
Description: New York : The New Press, 2016.
Identifiers: LCCN 2015030910| ISBN 9781620971758
    (hardback) | ISBN 9781620971765 (e-book)
Subjects: | BISAC: FICTION / Literary.
Classification: LCC PK2418.K838 K6313 2016 |
    DDC 891.4/6371—dc23 LC record available at
    http://lccn.loc.gov/2015030910

The New Press publishes books that promote and enrich public
discussion and understanding of the issues vital to our democracy
and to a more equitable world. These books are made possible
by the enthusiasm of our readers; the support of a committed
group of donors, large and small; the collaboration of our many
partners in the independent media and the not-for-profit sector;
booksellers, who often hand-sell New Press books; librarians;
and above all by our authors.

www.thenewpress.com

Typeset in Garamond Regular by SÜRYA, New Delhi

Printed in the United States of America

10   9   8   7   6   5   4   3   2   1

Author's dedication
For Umesh

Translator's dedication
To boatmen of every kind

Contents

Tanay

That you should not be here when something we've both wanted happens is no new thing for me. Today too, as always, you're not here.

The house is quiet. I'm alone at home. For a while, I basked in bed in the shifting arabesques of light diffusing through the leaves of the tagar. Then I got up slowly, and went down to the backyard, and sprawled on the low wall for a single moment. The silence made me feel like a stranger in my own home.

I walked around the house quietly, as a stranger might. The chirping of sparrows filled the kitchen. The other rooms were quiet, empty, forsaken. In the front room, the newspaper lay like a tent in the middle of the floor, where it had been dropped. At the door, a packet of flowers to appease the gods and a bag of milk.

Then I realized I was not alone. From their photograph, Aaji and Ajoba eyed me in utter grandparental disbelief. I took my coffee to the middle room window and sat down. That girl with the painful voice in the hostel next door? How come she's not shrieking about something?

To savour each bitter and steaming sip of coffee in such quiet?

That you should not be there when something we've both wanted happens is no new thing for me. Today too, as always, you're not here.

When you came into our lives, I was in a strange frame of mind. I would have been willing to befriend anyone my age. I was ready for friendship with someone who only read management books; or someone who was studying information technology; or someone who wanted to settle in the United States. Anyone.

You came as a paying guest. You gave my parents the rent. You gave me so much more. Then you slipped away.

Those shrill girls in the hostel next door,

weren't they keeping an eye on us? I'm now going to sit on the wall, and when my coffee's drunk, I'm going to scrape the dried coffee off the rim and the squelch at the bottom of the mug with a fingernail and then I'm going to lick it off. When that's done, I'm going to take off my shirt and continue to sit here.

One of the fundamental rights of mankind should be that of wearing as many or as few clothes as one likes inside one's own home. Or one should be able to wear none at all. Wasn't the eye that the shrill girls in the hostel kept on us an invasion of our privacy, an abrogation of our rights?

After a bath in cold water, you would wrap a towel around yourself and sit on the low wall, bringing with you the smell of soap. It was you who broke my habit of going straight down for breakfast after bathing and getting fully dressed.

Another of my habits you broke: my daily accounts. I'd write them down faithfully. Rs 40 for coffee; Rs 100 for petrol.

'Why keep accounts?' you asked once.

'It's a good habit. You should know where you're spending your money and on what.'

'What do you get from knowing that?'

I asked Baba the same question in the night.

Baba's answer was so stupid, I felt a spurt of sympathy for Aai. That night, I went for a walk and ate a paan; and I did not write down how much I spent on it.

Another first.

We hit it off immediately; neither of us liked the kind of girl who would sing syrupy light classical music—bhav geet; nor the kind of boy who would wear banians with sleeves. There was another thing I didn't like: marriage. And the many relatives who made it their business to discuss the subject ad nauseam. You had no relatives.

We would both have liked this moment. We knew that it would be ours one day. But it is now mine alone.

When I woke up, my eyes opened peacefully. I

felt the kind of peace you feel when you come in from a hot afternoon and pour cold water over your feet. When I opened my eyes, the day stretched before me, free of anxiety. When I opened my eyes, nothing was left of the night's anxieties. My eyelids floated up. To wake quietly from a deep sleep is a rare thing and, when it happens, you can almost imagine that the world had begun again, at least for a few seconds. Or so you said.

Watching me wake up one day, you asked, 'Why those frown lines? This look of pain?' Once when I watched you wake up, you had the same frown. You said, 'When one gets up, there's a moment when everything looks odd and strange.'

I let it go at that.

Today, when I woke up, my eyes drifted open. I felt the kind of peace you feel when you come in from a hot afternoon and pour cold water over your feet. But when I was making coffee a line inscribed itself on my forehead; and I began to think: Why this peace? Shouldn't I be crying? Throwing a tantrum? Complaining to someone?

Your stuff was all over the room: cloth bags, easel, guitar, books, cassettes, camera, Walkman, rolled-up canvases, and a book of pasta recipes. Baba had finished his fifth cup of tea. Aai was making the sixth. Aseem was in bed.

Anuja stopped the rickshaw at the door and got out; and, as is her wont, shouted three times, loudly, for change. Was that the first time you saw each other? When you took the ten-rupee note to her? Anuja shook your hand firmly, no doubt hurting your fingers. Aai introduced you over lunch: 'This is Anuja, Aseem and Tanay's sister.'

In the next two years, how much did you find out about my sister, a girl whose idea of fun was a strenuous trek to a fort, who grinds your fingers in a painful grip when she shakes your hand, who snores a little in her sleep, who listens with complete attention as if you were the last person in the world?

But that's my Anuja. Who is your Anuja? When did you get to know her? How? And how could I have been so blind right up to the end?

When you were giving Anuja the ten rupees, I was up in the tower room, picking up the shirt you had dropped, inhaling your scent from it. When you came up, I was looking through your albums. I hadn't even thought of it as an invasion of privacy. You came up behind me and put a hand on my shoulder and said quietly, 'That was taken a couple of days before the accident; the last photo.' My Marathi-medium school had not taught us to say, 'I'm sorry for your loss' at such moments. I hope I took hold of your hand then and gripped it tight.

Can a single day bear the burden of so many random firsts?

You spent all your Diwali vacations with uncles of various stripes. You ate your meals in hostel messes and, at each new halt, you found a roadside stall at which you could get your morning tea. You made yourself at home easily when you lived with us. It must not have been new, this living as a paying guest.

I had had my eye on that room, a dark one but well ventilated. Its main attraction was that it had its own access. I had assumed that it would be mine when I grew up. I would be able to come and go as I pleased. I would paint it the colours I wanted; decorate it the way I wanted. I would sleep in it, alone. But of course, that was the very room that my parents decided would attract a paying guest. And so I had showed this room to many potential residents, my face dark with resentment.

When I was a schoolboy, this was the room of my grandparents' illness. There were two low cots ranged against opposite walls, my grandmother on one, on the other my grandfather. Then only grandmother remained, the room suffused with the smell of Amrutanjan. After she had suffered all her karmic share of suffering, phenyle drove out the other smells: of the ageing body and drying behada bark, of supari and medicine. But the smell of Amrutanjan lingered.

When you came to see it, you said, 'What a tempting aroma this room has. Do you come here to sneak cigarettes?'

That's when I realized that smell is a matter of the mind. What smells you brought with you! Rum and cigarettes, your sweat and macaroni cooking on the hotplate, and then, because I loved it, attar of khus. And the smell of you, a unique personal smell of your own. When I think of you, that smell comes flooding back.

You came into the room and said, 'What a tempting aroma this room has.' I thought, if this chap takes the room, things might get interesting. I filled my chest with the smell of the room. Then you said, 'Do you come here to sneak cigarettes?' I realized that smell is a matter of the mind. Nothing is real.

As we chatted, sitting on the window ledge, in the middle of the night, I became aware of the mediocrity, the ordinariness of my secure and comfortable life.

You lost your parents when you were still in the tenth standard. You were offered the option of staying with relatives but chose to live in a hostel instead. You decided to live alone, to be independent, to make your own decisions. And through all this, the grim decision never to let a single tear fall.

When the results were declared, you did well. The crowd of happy parents made you uncomfortable and you slipped away. At the time, you were living with one of your aunts and you made your way home. The door was locked. Everyone had gone out. You sat on the sun-warmed steps, mark sheet in hand, and waited until evening . . . when you told me this, were those steps still warm for you?

Midnight in the window, just you and me. Even then you didn't cry. At these times, I felt I should be your mother, your father, your brother, your friend, everything. But you had long reached the point at which you decided you would never cry again.

The mattress I had brought up, saying that I would study in the tower room, was never taken downstairs again. I encroached on your space slowly, hoping not to be rebuffed at each new foray.

One night, when everyone had fallen asleep after dinner, I came upstairs and found you in my beige kurta, sketching me. I got it: you didn't mind my stealthy incursions. I also figured out that when the sketch was done, you were going to place it under my pillow. I slipped out again, closing the door behind me quietly and sat at the foot of the staircase, inhaling the scent of the raat rani.

The air was still. There was a light on in the kitchen, then the scrape of Baba's cough and the light went out. The girls' hostel across the road was still active. Some girls were oiling their hair and giggling. The rest were playing antakshari. Idly, I wondered what would happen to these foolish girls.

The light went out in the tower room. I went up and opened the door and approached the mattress. You were curled up on one side; the other a place for me, an invitation. Under the pillow, your sketch of me. But it wasn't the one I had seen. This one had me, the staircase and the raat rani.

When I looked carefully at you, I could see you had screwed up your eyes like a child pretending to sleep.

When we lost a one-act play competition, I sat on the hot steps of the theatre and wept as a child would, sobbing and gasping. You sat down next to me and drew me close and once again I felt we were back in the window, back in the middle of a cool night.

Two days after you left with Anuja, Baba ransacked your room. One moment he was drinking tea; the next he was on his feet, calling Aseem as he marched upstairs. Aai and I followed him, at a run.

There wasn't much in the room. From outside the window, we watched as Aseem and he turned what was left upside down. I had no energy left to speak, to intervene, to think. That pile of stuff reminded me of your first day here and my eyes filled. Aai thought I was crying because I was missing Anuja and she hugged me. Baba found nothing: no notes or slips of paper, no telephone diaries, no addresses, nothing that would fill out your context. No one saw how much of the stuff that they had tossed on to the floor was mine.

When they left, I saw four or five black-and-white photographs I had taken of you, peeping from a file. They'd faded a little over time and were stuck to each other. Delicately, I separated them.

When I took my Pentax out carefully from my bag, the rain had stopped. Soaked to the skin, you were looking at the sky, close to a black boulder washed clean by rainwater. You began to wipe your face with your sleeve and I stopped you, mid-wipe. You can see the glow of the rainwater and the gentle sun in the photograph.

You were about to finish a new painting. You had been at it day and night. In that riot of colour, I now see a cage. It isn't my face in the cage, but it resembles mine. That night when I came up to the terrace, you drew me greedily to you. And dark patches of colour sprang up over my body: red and yellow and the purple-black of the jamun. Irritated, I upended your wooden palette over your head and then, in the middle of the night, by lamplight, I took a picture of your colour-streaked face.

I stuck a few of those pictures up on the wall in my room below as well. But I didn't want anyone to be suspicious so I added random pictures of some college friends around them, one of my parents, and one of Anuja as a bawling baby. That night, Aseem came to sleep in the room. He locked the door and lit a cigarette at the window. He turned to me and said, 'Tomorrow I'll get you a picture of Sai Baba. Stick that up as well. Spoil all the walls with Sellotape marks.' When all this got to me, I would wonder whether I should ask you to leave with me, to go and stay somewhere else, somewhere far away.

But then I'd suddenly feel that I should ask you what you want to do with your life. Do you want a relationship? Would you dare?

I took two textbooks and started to come upstairs. I tried to be as quiet as possible but, when I went into the next room, I could hear Aai and Baba talking about something. They were speaking softly as they did when something was worrying them. Hearing my footsteps, they stopped. Aai wiped her eyes; Baba adjusted his expression and said, 'What happened? Not sleepy? Want me to rub oil on your head?' I didn't think I could come upstairs right away. I'll tell you about it later, I thought. When I took my Pentax out, the rain had stopped. You were wet through. Soaked to the skin, you were looking at the sky, close to a black boulder washed clean by rainwater.

I watched you through the lens. The cold made my hands tremble and the frame trembled too. At that moment, I felt I had to tell you what

I felt, devil take the consequences. Then you wiped your face with your sleeve and I stopped you, mid-wipe.

When you arrived, I was ready to be friends with the kind of person who read management books, studied computer software and wanted a green card. I was bored of the same old stories and the same old people. I would have been willing to befriend anyone my age. Anyone. Those first few days, at the start of term, were quiet, peaceful, as you were. That might have been because the idea of a lifelong partnership, a long-term commitment hadn't crossed my mind.

Shrikrishna Pendse was a boy like any other in our class; but when school reopened after the Diwali vacations one year, there was something different about him. He left the top button of his shirt open. His eyes were intense; and when he threw his arm around my shoulders, the smell of his body was seductive. Before school, after school, when the classroom emptied because everyone else was going to the laboratory, we grabbed at every opportunity to grab at each other. In that time between the ninth and the tenth standard, we began to rediscover ourselves. I couldn't sit still, I couldn't stay at home. The months passed in a haze of Euclidean geometry, Shrikrishna's chatter, full marks in mathematics and the slow growth of down on Shrikrishna's chest.

By contrast, our lovemaking was beautiful. At around three thirty in the morning, you slowly took me into your arms and I realized that this was the first time I had allowed this physical bliss to burgeon slowly. With Shrikrishna, there had always been an element of roughness. Was someone watching us? Would someone wake up? And then the habit of silence. And between you and Shrikrishna, how many different bodies! Twenty-five? Thirty? But they were all pretty much the same, and often it didn't matter if I didn't see their faces.

Once when I visited his house, Shrikrishna

was in the bathroom. His mother told me to wait in his room. With nothing to do, I opened a magazine lying on the table. Madhuri Dixit was featured in a swimming costume. Some nights later, as he was about to come, Shrikrishna closed his eyes and mumbled, 'Sheetal.' Sheetal was a girl in the second year. At that time I only felt slightly surprised.

Once after a bath, I opened the door of my cupboard to get a change of clothes. Just the day before, Ashwin Lele had got hold of a video cassette. It was not the kind you got easily. You had to know someone at the video library. Then, you had to have the house to yourself. Lele knew someone and his parents had gone off to their village. He had a cassette player. After class, everyone gathered at his house. I laughed uncomfortably as we watched. All the boys were trying to sound sophisticated. I took my clothes out of the cupboard and looked at myself in the mirror. I dropped the wet towel. I took a long, clear-eyed look at myself. That I was different was nowhere apparent.

In school, the question was unimportant. In college all my close friends were women. The other boys and girls did seem to get together, they did go out together, they rehearsed plays together and even went out of town on trips together. But it was only when it came to arranging the annual college day—who to invite, what to get—that I first went to Rashmi's home. No event in senior college seemed complete without Rashmi. Through the year, she didn't actually join any of the extracurricular activities of the college: not the literary circle and not the singing group; she was not part of the trophy-hungry theatre group and was not in the National Cadet Corps. But if any of these clubs had an activity or an event, Rashmi was sure to be part of it. She seemed to be able to talk to teachers and caterers, to lighting men and sound technicians, to the student union and even the principal. This was the same man who didn't even look up when he spoke to students but he would stop to chat with her before getting into his car and driving away. Often I didn't understand the behaviour of the girls around. (Still don't.) I saw Anuja as one of the few sensible girls I knew. All the others seemed conventional; they were the kind who would have to be 'proposed to', they would have to get home by seven in the evening, they would weep as they sang the kind of syrupy bhav geet that would bring tears to the eyes of the senior citizenry whose own children were settled in America.

When I first went to her house, it was about 11.30 in the morning. I knocked and waited for some minutes. Then I began to call her name. A little girl came out of a neighbouring flat. 'Hey,' she called and beckoned. I turned to her but she ran back into her flat and closed the iron security door. Sticking her nose out through the bars, she said: 'What's the use? Rashmitai must be still asleep. When I ring her number, the phone wakes her up.' She giggled at this and ran inside. The phone began to ring in Rashmi's flat. In a while, Rashmi came to the door, sleep clouding her eyes. She took the papers from my hand. To the little girl who had reappeared at the grill, she said, 'Cheene, your Aai is going to be late. Don't open the door to anyone. And come by in the afternoon for bread and jam.' Then she took the papers, thanked me and both Cheenoo and she slammed their doors.

Now I have a key to Rashmi's flat.

You didn't seem very curious about people. I'm different. After I got to know you, I wanted to know every little detail about you. Where did you go to school? Did you ever fall in love? With whom? How do you manage alone? What do you plan on doing? I would ask a flurry of questions and I would volunteer a flurry of details about myself.

I don't know how you managed it: an intense relationship with me, an attraction to Anuja, and then to leave with her? To live somewhere else?

Yesterday, Ashish and Samuel invited me over for a meal. Both their names were on the door. Ashish was cooking while Samuel helped, unobtrusively. They refused to let me do anything. I sat on a stool in the kitchen and watched them at work. I think they deliberately chose not to mention you. After lunch, while we were having coffee, Ashish went and sat next to Samuel and placed his warm cup against Samuel's cheek. I looked down immediately. Samuel saw my discomfiture and said, 'I'll get some cookies,' and went into the kitchen.

In the last couple of years, I have begun to feel the need for a permanent relationship, something I can grow into. The thought had crept up on me that I might have such a relationship with you. When I looked at my parents and thought about this whole 'together forever' thing, it never struck me as anything exciting. Yesterday, I was a little envious of what Samuel and Ashish had. When she spoke of Aseem's wedding, Aai always said, 'It's best if these things happen in good time.' In her world, unmarried men were irresponsible, free birds and unmarried women like Rashmi had 'not managed to marry'.

What do two men who decide to live together do? Men like you and me? Those who don't want children? Those who don't have the old to look after or the young to raise? No one would visit us because we'd be living together as social outcasts. For most of the day, we would do what we liked.

You sometimes asked me, 'Why do you stare at me like that?' Did you know what I was thinking? We hadn't met Samuel and Ashish then so I didn't know any male couples who lived together.

You spoke of a couple who had never lived together. She was a French writer whose work you loved. He was also a writer and a philosopher. They had never lived under the same roof. But they were friends and had remained so. Throughout their lives, they had pooled in their income. They did an impressive amount of writing, teaching and fighting for the causes they valued. They had given themselves the right to create a new kind of relationship. You spoke animatedly about them; the second time

you described their relationship, I said, 'You've
told me about this already.'

'I'll get some cookies,' Samuel said and went
into the kitchen. Ashish and I sat there without
speaking.

Samuel did not come back. Perhaps he'd gone
for a nap. After a while, Ashish came and sat
down next to me. He said, 'It hurts, doesn't it? I
get it.' But it was he who began to cry. I hugged
him and patted his back as he cried and cried.
Finally, exhaustion set in and he stopped and
wiped his reddened eyes.

He said, 'Don't worry about it. Sometimes, I
don't understand Samuel at all. There are these
phone calls that go on for hours on end. And if
I'm with him, he goes into the next room. I just
look at him. What can I say?'

For hours on end, I sat in that upstairs room,
staring at you while you went about your life,
unaware of my attention. You would be
squeezing paint out of tubes, hanging your
clothes out to dry, wiping your stained hands on
your T-shirt, blowing on the milk as it bubbled

over, lifting vessels off the hotplate, or sucking
on a singed finger. I'd be staring at you and
thinking, I should ask, I should ask, I should
ask: do you want to be in a stable monogamous
relationship for the rest of your life?

Even if we're not going to have children,
even if we don't have to worry about guests,
even if we're going to end up sleeping on two
single beds, separated by a table on which there's
a copper vessel containing water, I want us to be
together.

Why? I was a child then. I woke up in the
middle of the night and went in search of a
glass of water. Aai had a fever and Baba was
sitting by her side, stroking her head. He gave
her her pills and then he helped her up and took
her to the bathroom . . . I still remember that
scene.

No one had made me want to ask that
question. Not Shrikrishna Pendse with whom I
stole some moments in empty classrooms; not
Amit Chowdhuri who lived alone behind Sharayu
Maushi's home; not Girish Sir who kept me

back after rehearsals when all the other kids had been sent away.

After we made love, I felt a delicious lassitude creeping over me. When consciousness returned, I realized that you were still with me; you hadn't turned your back and edged away.

Later, I was awakened by the warmth of the sun, filtering in through the window, and a delectable aroma in the air. It was you, after a bath, your hair wet, sitting in a chair, looking at me.

'Why the lines on your forehead? Why that look of pain?' I cleared my face, consciously letting happiness through.

A thought: what if the ground were glass? I would be able to see a bunch of friends talking about their children. And Aseem's hidden stash of *Debonair* with its photographs of topless women would fall out from among his books. A cousin was being gheraoed by a circle of relatives; he had published his mental and physical needs in the newspapers. Now it's Aseem's turn, they shout. Now Tanay's. In the other room, Aai and her friends are looking at the jewellery that has been reserved for Anuja. Aai tells her friends that she has been scrupulously fair: whatever she has made for Anuja, she has had identical pieces made for her future daughters-in-law. In the next room, two colossal cradles have been hung. In them are two babies whose naming ceremonies are about to commence. Ashwini's husband of three days cannot take his eyes off me. The turbulence of ritual swirls through the house. The women are jostling for place and for priority. When I see Ashwini's husband standing near the dark wall of the station, he blushes and laughs. Having trapped the woman who has delivered herself of two children and grown fat, the men dance in a ring in a maidan. Happiness, happiness, everywhere happiness. Even the woman who has had two children and has grown fat is happy.

I want to go and say something in each of these places and see what effect it has. But in this kerfuffle, who will hear my voice? So I sit silently in a corner. It occurs to me just as suddenly: what if everyone suddenly looks up, through the transparent glass ceiling, at us?

I woke again—Baba shouting for me. I drew the curtain on the hostel side. I sorted out my clothes from yours and slipped into them and ran downstairs. I thought I was going to be upbraided for laziness, for sleeping until eleven. But it wasn't that. It was only that the prasad he had brought from the Swami of Akalkot had not been sent across to the Ranade family. Mischievously, he said, 'This is your punishment.' Then he pushed a cup of not-very-good tea into my hands. When I drank it, he told me he had made it himself. From scratch. Sting was singing 'Fields of gold' deliriously from Anuja's room. Aai was making onion thaalipeeth. The first one went to Aseem, as it always did. As he ate it, he looked at me and laughed.

Perhaps the night had gone well for everyone.

Everyone reacts differently to alcohol. Quiet men shout their protests against the world. The aggressive turn humble and polite. It's different with you; alcohol makes you ask questions, the odd questions only you can ask.

When your glass was empty, you picked up an ice cube and began to look at me through it. You did this fairly often because my glass was usually empty as were the bottles. Then you rubbed the cube on your face, on your eyelids and you asked, 'So tell me. Why do you call your city the cultural capital of the state?' I tried to remember what we had learned in school: that there were some great colleges here, and a famous university that attracts students from across the country, from across the world. We had some of the state's finest writers, poets, musicians, singers and the like. You had to win the approval of the audience in this city to prove yourself.

But of course, to us, culture is anything that is more than a hundred years old. We are rather worried about keeping our culture alive. In order to do so, almost everyone has started some kind of cultural organization. There is a river that runs through the city. Those who want their culture to survive and those who want it to change live on different sides of the river. That the Ganeshotsav started by Tilak should be kept alive is a given. When the palkhis go through the city, young girls wearing nine-yard saris sing songs on special television programmes. There are laavnis and other traditional dances at mass meetings.

This is it: we present an account of ourselves in our art forms. Every family seems to have a member who lives in America or one who is acting in a television serial based on a classic novel. And so this city is called the cultural capital of the state.

In the middle of the city runs a river. When I was in school, there were only three bridges across the river. Today, there are nine. When this otherwise thin trickle of a river swells into a torrent of tea-coloured water, Anuja, Aseem, Baba and I would go to look at it. We'd lean against the bridge and watch the drama of water and mud. It's been a long time since the river filled up like that.

A road runs by the river and then turns left to run past the station. At the end of the road is my college. Through classes eleven and twelve, I was oblivious of it but some time during my first year of senior college, I realized what was going on along that road. It must have been one of those days when I was returning home late from rehearsals. I could see men standing along the road, each maintaining a certain distance from the other. Almost all of them turned to look at me, as I passed by on my bike. Within some weeks, I had gone with one of them to his home, with another to the five-star hotel in which he was staying. I had no idea how to satisfy the hungers of my body. Perhaps many of them didn't know either. I struck up conversations with some of them. Some of them had married out of fear of their families. Some came from other cities, seeking a night of love. Some were truly lost; they had stopped caring what they were doing.

In a few months, it occurred to me that I seemed to have lost all fear. I would slow down until the bike was crawling along the road. Some young man would walk up and offer his hand. If I liked him, I would ask him his name, tell him the pseudonym I had invented for these encounters. The next question was always the same: 'Got a place we can go?' I would say no. If he had somewhere we could go, he would climb onto the bike and we'd go there. There was no money involved. We pleasured each other for the pleasure of giving pleasure. After that, I would be empty of any feeling, except for a loathing of my body. I would go into the bathroom and scrub myself clean. I would wonder why I was doing this.

After Aaji died, the parents decided to use the upstairs room for a paying guest. It took them some time to make up their minds. Aseem was ready for marriage, Aai said, and it should be kept for him and given to him and his wife. But when Nadkarni Kaka built a girls' hostel in his large yard and began to earn money, Baba began to feel the need to turn his home into a paying proposition.

Aai told Aseem all this as she tied his tie one morning. He listened without comment. The next morning, he tied his tie himself and announced that he was thinking of buying a small flat of his own.

The morning after that, Aai told Baba about this and they decided to rent the room out. Without actually discussing it, they decided that the paying guest should be a man. It said so in the advertisement they put in *Mid-Day*. Perhaps they thought complications might arise if a girl were to be allowed into the house what with me and Aseem on the loose. Anuja added another dimension to this. 'Let's not have a woman. The Nadkarnis won't like it; competition to their girls' hostel.' The ad also stated the time of the day when the room might be viewed. Only Aai and I would be at home at those times. I showed the room to four or five other men before you came along.

Priyadarshan Majumdar was the first to reply to our ad. He came home in the afternoon, and I took him upstairs. He was about five and a half foot tall and had spectacles on. He had a carefully groomed stubble and could not have been more than twenty-two or twenty-three but he affected the air of a mature man. He didn't like anything about the tower room. Not the independent access, not the walls so thick that a full-grown man could sit on the window ledge. He didn't care for the breeze, not for the chaafa tree that grew so close it practically forced its flowers on you, not the bathroom that he wouldn't have to share, not even the bevy of girls from Nadkarni's hostel. When he did not call for many days afterwards, I began to assume that the tower room was going to be mine.

About a week later, a young man from Chandigarh who had just joined a multinational wanted to see the room. With him, he had brought a young woman whose face was largely obscured by a pair of dark glasses. He liked almost everything about the room. Not bothered that I was there, he waltzed her round the room, holding her hand. When Baba said at dinner that they were married and were going to get a flat of their own and needed our room as a bridge residence, Aai was brusque. 'We don't have to be anyone's bridge residence, please. And certainly not that type of person. I can see her now, coming and going at all hours. Besides, who can be sure she is his wife?'

When you came, I wasn't at home. At dinner again, Aai announced, 'I see no objection to letting this one have the room. He has good manners. I like him. He has no parents. I think he translates from French or something. He's studying art in the third year. He's coming to take another look tomorrow. This Tanay had taken the keys and marched off so I couldn't show the room to him.'

When I opened the door the next day, you were wearing a battered off-white T-shirt and faded jeans. You walked up the stairs in front of me. I opened the room and you stepped in and picked up a cobweb lying on the floor and threw it out of the window. I opened the other windows as you wandered around the room. Then you began to mutter, 'Here the bed. There the deck. And a satranji in the window. The books go there and in that niche behind the cupboard, the hotplate. What do you think?'

I shrugged. And thought, 'Lucky fucker. A whole room to yourself.'

Then I saw that you were still looking at me. You walked up to me and took me by the upper arm and squeezed.

'Good biceps. Gym every day?'

'Yes,' I said.

Then you stretched out your arms and said, 'What a tempting aroma this room has.'

We didn't bother much about caste and such matters at home. But when we sat down to dinner and you asked Aai for a poli, I could see her perk up. Brahmins say 'poli' while other castes make do with the humble 'chapatti'— same bread, different brand name.

Baba took the bull by the horns.

'May I ask who is your family god?' he asked.

You said, 'You don't have to be so formal, Uncle.'

'No, no, who does the family worship?'

You sat back and quietly finished the mouthful you had begun to eat. Then you said, 'I begin from myself. I have no home, no caste, no clan. I have kept my relatives at arm's length. I do not know who I believe in. I am a seeker.'

Perhaps Aai made sense of this because she stopped the interrogation in its tracks. I could see that Baba didn't understand what you had said. So he tried another tack: 'Where does your family come from?'

'Where I am, that's where I come from.'

Then you turned to Aai and said, 'Kaku, the aamti is excellent. Did you put ghee in the daal when it was boiling?'

Aai began to tell you the recipe and the topic changed.

Generally, every surname brought with it a hundred questions for people like my parents. If I brought a friend home and introduced him a name was never enough.

'Aai, this is my friend Rohan.'

'Rohan? Rohan what? Does he have any other

name? Do you find it terribly difficult to introduce your friends with their full names?'

Once that cat was out of the bag, then she'd be able to see some special features in his face. Or not.

That you don't use any surname at all seemed odd to me at first. I thought it was some form of artistic licence. But then you said that the only name that had any meaning was the one that someone used when they wanted to call out to you. And I saw the vanity of the surname through your eyes. As I began to think like you, eventually I began to wonder what I should do with my father's name and surname.

You thumped me one and said, 'If you have a surname, keep it. There are hundreds of Tanays. How will you stand out from them?'

'And you want to stay in the shadows?'

'If I find someone whose surname I want to share, I'll add it to my name.'

In my head, I tried your name with our common-or-garden Joshi attached.

Once you asked me to soap your back. I took

off my T-shirt and rolled my trousers up to the
knees. I washed your back and then came out,
rolled my trousers down again and put on my
T-shirt. Then I sat down at the table and began
reading.

I realized that I had gradually stopped going
to the station road, stopped visiting chat rooms.
And this despite the fact that we didn't even
hold hands for days. As I sat there reading, I
glanced back to see you standing at the mirror,
drying your hair. It occurred to me then that the
change had happened of itself, on its own. You
were there all the time. You were mine alone. Or
so I thought.

In my head I united our names, inscribed
them on a brass plate and attached them to a
mahogany door that you had carved. Our door
was the most beautiful in the entire building.
Everyone would know what a creative person—
with a bright, cool, clear mind—lived behind
that mahogany door. When we discovered that
we wanted the same colours on the walls, we
high-fived each other. But it couldn't have been

any other way. I hadn't given much thought to colour before you came into our lives. You wanted a wood floor; the last room would be your studio. Our doors would always be open to our friends: some theatre people, some artists. When Aai and Baba dropped in on us, a surprise visit, they always wondered why we took so much time to open the doors. That was because we had seen them through the peephole and we'd rushed about, taking down the nudes you'd just finished from the walls. And as soon as we opened the door, one of them would say, 'Why does it always take you hours to open the door? Why lock the door anyway? Who's coming to steal your stuff?'

On her way to put down all her dabbas in the kitchen, Aai would add, 'Now that you're doing all this, the least you could do is learn to wipe the counters properly, no?' Then she would wipe them herself.

In front of the bedroom balcony, I wanted a chaafa tree of the same profusion and invasiveness as the one that pushed into the tower room. You planted it immediately. When I complained that the building in front of us obstructed my view of the sunrise, you magicked it out of the way. We argued up a storm with the plumber. He had no idea that we wanted each tap to flow with a different colour of water. Only the tap in the kitchen would be different: it would have a steady supply of ice-cold beer. When he stepped back after he finished fitting the tap and demonstrating the flow of beer, I realized that he had Aseem's face. He said, 'Saahab, you wanted it so I've put in a beer connection. But you should know that too much beer and your sperm count suffers.'

I would dream this house into existence as I was falling asleep, in the haze before of an afternoon nap. We hadn't met Ashish and Samuel then. I thought that it was going to be difficult, trying to live together. But then the city was getting used to difference. Heterosexual live-in relationships were permitted. And there were those who chose to live alone. Our ward's councillor was a bigamist. There was a famous brothel behind the market. There were hijras for hire at almost every traffic signal. If people weren't precisely proud of these things, at least they knew about them. So how was I any different?

When I was young, as if by unspoken agreement, the entire family would descend on us for the vacations. At first, everyone came to us for ten days, then all the children would go to Nasik for a week with Aatya and then for four or five days we would go to Ram Kaka. The last one or two days of this trip were spent with Prakash Kaka.

This was how the holidays were spent. When everyone was with us, one of the most important events was the making of ice cream by hand. Ice, milk, salt, mango pulp would all be mixed together, with everyone taking a turn at churning. You gave up only when your arms began to hurt. By four or four thirty in the afternoon, mango ice cream would be ready and we would eat until we were forced to decline any more helpings. No one was supposed to mention it again for the rest of the month.

On one of those days, I was taking the wooden ice cream bucket out of the kitchen when Sunil, Ram Kaka's son, hit me on the legs. I almost dropped the bucket. I sat down to rub my legs. Sunil was always exercising; he could talk about nothing other than his body and his exercises. He shouted, 'Walk properly. Keep your legs apart and walk straight. Why do you mince along like a woman?' Then he took me into the backyard which was set with large square tiles. He forced me to spread my legs apart—and place my feet in separate tiles. Then he made me walk with my legs apart. For about an hour, he sat on Baba's scooter and tried to rewrite my gait.

'Tannya, walk straight, don't trip about like a girl, keep those shoulders up, push your chest out,' he roared. Aai was in the kitchen scraping the meat out of coconuts and he told her, 'Kaku, make him walk like this every morning and send him out to play with the boys. He just sits around reading.'

From then on, right up to this day, I fear that I walk funny, in other words, that I walk like a woman. When I find myself walking at my own pace, I almost immediately slow down. And I learned what men do not do. They do not wet their dry lips by running their tongues over them. They don't trot after their mothers into the kitchen. They don't use face powder. They don't sit on a motorbike behind a woman. They don't need mirrors in the rooms where they might change their clothes. On trips, they can go behind a tree. They don't even need an enclosed space to take a dump; they can do it in the open. They shouldn't be afraid of other people seeing their bodies. If there's only one bathroom, they can bathe in the open. When caned in class, they do not cry. They do not buy tamarind from the lady who sells it on the road and they certainly do not sit by her side and eat it.

This dates back to the time before you came to live with us, about four or five months before your arrival. I was reading the paper when I recognized the face of a man who had killed himself. I had gone with him once to his bungalow.

One night at the station road, there weren't too many men on offer. There was, however, a large car standing at the edge of the road. Leaning against the bonnet was a man in his early forties, tall, slim, with a gym-built body. The station road had become part of my routine. When I arrived, he was already there. When I saw him, I slowed down and stopped right in front of him. We left together in his car. Even though it was his own house, he seemed to be afraid. Would the watchman wake up? Would the gate creak? The house was large; I think he had a military post of some kind but he lived alone in that huge bungalow. He asked me to sit down when we went in. He brought me a can of beer from the fridge. Then he went away, changed his clothes and came back. He took me to a bedroom upstairs. There was a fridge and a bar tucked away behind a glass door. For a long time, he wandered around the room and I sat on the bed, watching him. Then he seemed to relax

a little and he came and sat down next to me and
put his hand on my shoulder. He pushed the
hair away from my forehead. Then he drew me
close and pulled my head into his lap. He began
to pat my head. For what felt like an hour. In the
beginning he was silent but then he began to
talk, almost to himself. He had slept with many
people, he said, but he had never found someone
to talk to. He loved children. He paid the fees
and expenses of his old retainer's grandson.
Now he was beginning to feel lonely. He had
not married and had tried to hide himself in the
military. He told me, 'At first the bodies of
young men excited me greatly. But that has
passed now. When I see someone of your age, I
think: I should have someone like that as a
partner. Someone I can call my own, someone
to worry about me. But now, at my age, who's
going to let me adopt a boy?' I just sat there,
listening to him. He kept stroking my hair. As I
listened, I felt a sadness grow inside me. Then
he brought me back to the station road. I gave
him my email address; for a few days after that,

I got email from him. I didn't know what to write back, so I let them go unanswered.

Now he had killed himself. I set the paper aside. His voice echoed in my ears. His loneliness was like a warning. I wondered: how long could I play this game of bodies? I needed to find someone with whom I could have a steady relationship.

Baba came and picked up the paper. He took it and sat down in the chair opposite. Aai brought him tea and said, 'If you'd care to listen, I was talking to Aseem about the upstairs room. He says now he's thinking of buying his own flat. So if you want to put that ad in the evening papers for a paying guest . . .'

Years ago, when Aaji was in charge, we paid strict attention to rituals. The family deity was in our care. That meant festivals and ceremonies had to be celebrated as much for Aaji as for the deity. When Aai had finished cooking, Aaji would take some of what was cooked, on banana leaves, to feed the cow that was tied up outside the temple. Sometimes, she'd take Anuja with her. She was scared of the traffic. If Anuja complained too much or wasn't home from school, I would have to go. There was no question of refusing; when Baba obeyed without protest, who were we to refuse?

For three or four days, Aai would sit in a room by herself. She would do no work. She would eat only the food Aaji cooked. Aaji would make everything herself, even the tea. I had no idea why Aai was in seclusion. I'd ask Baba but he wouldn't answer. All I knew was that she could touch no one and no one could touch her. She even looked different during that time, as if she were a guest in her own home. I would go into her room and sit on a mat and stare at her. Once when she was sleeping, I crept up and touched her body gently. Nothing happened. She looked beautiful and fresh. All day long, she would lie there, reading magazines. Then on the fifth day, she would be up and about, doing her work. Her hair would be wet. But when Aaji fell

down the stairs, Aai stopped incarcerating herself
for those days.

When you left suddenly, I felt somewhat as I
had felt when I watched Aai sitting alone in her
room. That day, it turned dark. And it began to
rain. I stood in the backyard, letting myself get
wet. You'll laugh, but for a moment, I even
heard the guitar playing in your room.

When I think about my childhood, I feel the
best times came before one began to seek
pleasure in the bodies of others.

When you're looking for a relationship, the
process weakens you. You feel you have to bear
with whatever the other person wants. This is
one of my basic beliefs about human nature.
Each one of the people I have met has made
this a little more clear.

Once when I came up to the tower room in
the middle of the night, you said, 'Would you
mind sleeping downstairs? I want to be alone
tonight.' Hurt, I turned to go. You saw this,

perhaps, and you said, 'If you want to chat a while, stay for a bit.' I couldn't bear your pity but I sat down anyway and found that my sense of belonging had evaporated. I said, 'Oh, is that the way it is?' You laughed and shrugged. You threw open your arms and hugged me close and stroked my back for a while. Then you let me go and said, 'Go, get some sleep.'

Disappointed, I came back to the house. I hoped you'd at least be at the door but when I looked up the light in your room was out. I said to myself: Don't disturb him. Enough. He wants to be alone.

I called Anuja. Cursing, she came and opened the door.

'What is it? What happened?' she asked. I said nothing and went in, locking the door behind me. 'Where did you go?' she kept at it. 'Upstairs?'

I nodded.

'Don't go and wake him up in the night. His eyes hurt sometimes because of his work.'

In my head I thought, why is she taking your side?

I snapped, 'No need for lectures. Go to sleep.'

'Hey, why are you fighting with me?' she said and rumpled my hair.

Insult added to injury. When Anuja put out her light, I opened the door and went upstairs again. I was about to knock on the door when I looked in at the window. You were sleeping on the floor, a sheet covering your body. You looked like some homeless person sleeping on a railway platform. I thought: Enough.

I didn't want to wake someone else up so I sat on the steps. And then a couple of firecrackers leapt into the sky and burst. They lit up everything for a moment and then went silent. Suddenly, from all four sides, crackers began to go off. Young men began to run down the road, roaring. From the hostel, someone shouted, 'Hey, Sonal, Shamita, we won, we won!' The screams and shouts almost drowned the sound of the crackers.

Slowly, everything settled down again. I could hear you coughing inside your room. I came to look in at you but you had turned on your side. I wanted to call to you, wake you up, ask you why you had turned me out. Perhaps if we talked things over, I wouldn't feel so bad. What do you mean, you want to be alone? It's me after all, so what's all this about privacy? How can you suddenly start behaving like this? What do you think of yourself?

Then you turned over again and once more I could see your face. I looked at you and I could do nothing.

Two days after you left, as he was drinking tea, a thought occurred to Baba. He got up and asked Aseem to come with him upstairs.

'And what are you lot up to?' Aai asked as she came into the courtyard.

I had been lying around doing nothing but I got up too and followed him. Baba opened the cupboards and began to throw their contents on to the floor. For a moment, Aseem was frozen, watching Baba go berserk. Then he too began to throw things around.

Many of the things they were treating so savagely were mine but they didn't know that. The upstairs room is still that way: books on the floor, canvases shredded. Blue paint has dried on the floor where a bottle broke. The lampshade you fashioned out of handmade paper is torn. I sometimes go and sit there. It is my museum of broken things.

Now that that idiot Anuja has come back alone, the whole family is absorbed in her. Until she returned, I was sure, when I sat in that room, that you had gone your separate ways. It was some weird coincidence that you had left on the same day. Anuja had been lured away by some fort, some mossy mountain ridge, some old house that had to be explored. Usually, she would tell someone and go; this time she had gone without telling anyone. I was sure that when she was done, she'd come back. That was her nature and I liked her for it. I pictured her living a free life somewhere else. 'I should go and see what's happening with the Narmada,' she'd say, 'better than sitting at home, reading about it in the papers.' I thought she had followed the protest against the dam on the river. Or she was climbing the Waghdarwaza at Raigarh.

In the morning, my museum is lit by a golden light. When it rains, drops of water leap into the room. Some of the colours on the canvases begin to flow as if wet. Then the night air dries them.

I couldn't imagine where you had gone.

In the last week, Menden told me that Mehnaz and Abbas are thinking of closing Sunrise down. On the day you disappeared, I ran to Sunrise when evening came but you didn't. Menden said you hadn't even come for breakfast. 'Did he say something about going to his village?' I asked. Mehnaz was standing at the counter, looking as if she were a lump of dough. She said that you had paid your bill a few days earlier.

When you come back, Sunrise will be no more. Mehnaz and Abbas are going back to Iran.

When I read you 'Pushkala', that iconic poem by Pu Shi Rege that describes a well-endowed woman, you said, 'Wait, I'll show you an actual Pushkala,' and you took me to Sunrise. I didn't even know we had a real Irani hotel in our city.

As we sat down on those polished round-bottomed chairs, Mehnaz appeared at the counter. She looked like a maiden of maida. I felt that Rege could well have been sitting where I was, when he wrote 'Pushkala'.

You waved to Mehnaz. I looked at the kitchen counter. Menden was slicing loaves of bread and buttering them. I slapped your shoulder and drew your attention to the clean, sharp lines of his handsome face. You grinned and raised your eyebrows.

I said, 'Let's have breakfast here every day.'

'Sure. As long as there's a handsome Christian waiter and Mehnaz—a sumptuous woman, a veritable Pushkala—always ready to sit for me, what else could a painter ask for?'

If we wanted Menden to serve us, we had to get one of the four tables that were in his corner. One morning, you said, 'When Menden comes to serve me, take a careful look. He's quite short. He has to bend over to put the plates on the table and then his cheek comes quite close.'

From that time on, we'd race each other from the signal near Sunrise to get to those chairs. Once, you plonked yourself down just before me. I didn't slow down in time and slammed into Menden. He fell over and I landed across him. Concerned, Abbas came up to help me and I winked at you.

When you return, there will be no Sunrise. Mehnaz and Abbas will have returned to Iran. Menden told me this in passing. I went home and took out a watercolour you had done of Mehnaz. When I came back with it, Abbas opened the counter flap and asked me upstairs.

The stairs were in a state of disrepair, the red carpet worn out in patches. Mehnaz served shikanjabin and Abbas and I sat at a round table in the middle room. I unrolled the painting in front of him and he sighed. 'He has magic in his hands,' he said.

Mehnaz brought me a chair and a glass jar, the big kind in which the biscuits were stored. 'He'd sit in this chair for ages, sketching. "You have so many chairs; sell me a couple, na?" he'd say. And he would stroke those jars when he came to pay his bill at the counter. A gift to remember Sunrise by,' she said.

I gripped Abbas's hand tight. I couldn't touch Mehnaz though I wanted to weep on her shoulder. I just smiled at her.

Menden helped me get the chair into a rickshaw. 'What about you?' I asked.

'McDonald's is coming here,' he said. 'I don't think they'll hire the likes of me. And no Udipi restaurant will take me. I'll go home to Trichy. Then I'll see how it goes.'

I set the chair down in the middle of the tower room. In a corner, by the window, I placed the glass jar. In the night, when I switch on the light, the chair swims into the half-light. And a distorted reflection of the room, as if seen through a wide-angle lens, appears on the sides of the jar.

Sometimes, I see Mehnaz, the flour doll, sitting on that chair. She's swathed in a burkha now, only her flushed cheeks and blue eyes visible. I see your hand, making slashes of blue and black on a canvas. I had no idea you were so deeply connected to so many people.

When you first decided to bask in the sun, clad only in shorts, the girls in the hostel began to murmur. And giggle. One of them, the one who always let down her wet hair so she could dry it on the balcony, came out, saw you, gasped 'Aiyya' and scuttled in again. You didn't seem to notice. With your Walkman plugged into your ears, you were lost to the world.

Slowly the girls who dried their hair in the balcony began to gather again. Shamita, Ground Floor, would come out and read Sartre in a marked manner. Sarika, Second Floor, would drop her towel or her kurta into our courtyard from time to time; you'd hand it back and accept her thanks quietly and go back to your music.

One day, the wind brought a bra and dropped it into our yard. You were listening to music, your eyes closed. I was washing my bike in the yard. When you opened your eyes, you saw the bra lying on the ground. You picked it up and waved it at the balcony load of girls.

'Excuse me. One of you looking for this?'

The balcony emptied immediately. Everyone scuttled off to their rooms. You waved the bra aloft and said, 'No one for this?' and then shrugged and hooked it on to the washing line. Silence. Shocked, I looked around. Just your luck. No one was around. I pictured the kind of expressions Nadkarni Kaku and Aai would have had, had they seen you waving a bra around. I didn't want to be called upon as a witness. I went into the house quickly.

I kept ducking Aai all day; she'd come into one room and I'd go into the other. In the afternoon I was lolling about, watching a film on Star Movies when Nadkarni Kaku called. I sat up immediately. Aai went to the washing line. Nadkarni Kaku began to talk, her head wiggling volubly.

Since it was my duty to run interference, I called, 'Aai, phone for you.' Aai came back into the house and said, 'Thank you.' She had a steel dabba in her hands—hot batata vadas. Nothing to worry about. When I came up after dinner, you'd already finished a quarter of Old Monk rum. You were sitting in the window, a loving look on your face. I curled up in the remaining space and we looked at each other and burst out laughing.

'What plastic women these are! Did you see them running in? Every item of clothing is important. I mean, any piece of clothing . . .' your voice tailed off.

'Yes? Any piece of clothing?'

'I know this may sound absurd . . .'

And you dissolved into laughter again.

I waved the empty bottle in front of you. 'Did you drink all of it then?'

You stopped laughing and said, 'Though it may sound absurd to you, no piece of clothing is more important than the others.' Then you yawned and added, 'They don't get this. So I don't get them. All the girls in college are like that. They scramble to look good. They want to be safe. Not my type. I like people who are basically good at heart . . . totally free. You can dialogue with them. I can adjust, I suppose. Now I won't go to bed with someone unless he's a friend. Being alone's a habit now. But I suppose I could break that too.'

You were already falling asleep as you spoke.

When I woke up suddenly in the middle of the night, I discovered you'd turned your back on me and moved away.

Yesterday, as she dropped me home, Rashmi said, 'I'm going to spring-clean tomorrow. Come and help?' I smiled and stuck my thumb into the air and went into the house. If you're asked something when you're reading a book, browning onions in the kadhai or otherwise occupied, you don't even raise your head. You just stick your thumb into the air if you want to say yes.

It's recently come to my attention that when I'm listening to someone, I cock my head. On the phone I hold the receiver between my head and my shoulder as Anuja does, playing a rhythm on the table in front of me. When I watch a film, I run my fist over my face, as Shrikrishna used to. When I shave, I bring my face close to the mirror, as Baba does. When the milk boils over, I walk to the gas range calmly, turn it off and wipe the counter down, without a word— as Aai does.

How did I acquire those habits? Perhaps that's what happens during the forging of a relationship: if nothing else, you adopt some of the other person's habits. It makes you feel those small adaptations, those adoptions, make him one of you.

Have you picked up some habits from me? Do you draw circles with a finger on your thali when you've finished eating? Do you, every once in a while, squeeze shaving cream on to your toothbrush? Do you sleep with a knee drawn up to you, the bedclothes kicked away?

Do you fold the newspaper neatly and put it where you found it, when you're done?

Yesterday, when a cobalt blue smudge of the wall ended up on my hand, I wiped it on my trousers without thinking.

Your habit of saying 'We'll see' irritated me immensely but I have to admit you deployed it skilfully and for the longest possible time. When Arindam sent his first email asking us to a meeting, I asked you if you would go with me.

'Let's see,' you said.

So I went out, knocked on the door and came in again, and said, 'Will you come with me to the meeting?'

You laughed and went to look for some clothes.

I hate the kind of person who keeps his options open until the last moment. It makes me angry.

'Say yes or no and let the person who's asking you go free,' I said to you.

'The person's free already.'

'Are you afraid to say "No"?'

'If I were to say "No", would you accept it without arguing?'

'Try it and see,' I said. 'Besides I'm arguing right now because your "Let's see" generally means "No".'

'If I don't change my ways, will things fall apart?' you asked.

At such times, I'd go thundering down the stairs. This was a tricky ploy. My plan was:

1. I thunder down the stairs.
2. You come after me. You apologize. You ask me to come back up.
3. I say, 'Buddy, you cannot be so self-centred in a relationship. You have to learn to make some compromises with your principles.'
4. You apologize again, you say that you get it, and instead of 'Let's see', you say 'Yes'.
5. We go out together.

Most times my plan failed at step one. I would come down the stairs and wander about in the house, waiting for you. I'd snarl at everyone and sulk in the kitchen.

Once I came down in just such a manner. I waited for you to follow. Twenty minutes later, the phone rang. I refused to answer. Naturally, no one else came to pick it up so finally I had to. It was some senior citizen from the French Institute, asking for you in a polite voice. I told Aai to call you and sat down near the phone, a frown scoring lines on my brow.

You took the phone and I heard half of the conversation: 'Hello? . . . Yes . . . Okay? . . . Let's see . . . I'm not sure . . . Maybe, yes . . . Okay . . . Okay . . . But that's not fixed yet . . . Okay . . . Bye.'

Then you turned to look at me and shouted to Aai, 'Kaku, don't you need to get the gas cylinder? This Tanay is just sitting here, shall I take him on the bike to get it?'

Aai bustled into the kitchen and said, 'Oh yes, that's right. It's a good thing you remembered. No one else in this house seems bothered. Tanay, come on, get up. Go and get a cylinder.'

I looked at you and shouted, 'Going, going.' Aai had no idea why I shouted so loudly.

Last week, I couldn't sleep and so I stepped into the courtyard. I sat down on the stones of the old washing area and looked up at the tower room. It began to drizzle, a thin but determined spray of droplets that wet me completely. I don't know how long I sat there. The sound of Baba's scooter startled me.

Anuja has been sent to Sharayu Maushi's for a change of scene. The parents had gone to see her. When they returned, Aai was weeping, the edge of her sari stuffed into her mouth. Baba simply took off his shoes and went into the house. I gathered Aai into my arms and tried to calm her down.

You would have liked the way I behave now. Your rules. Don't let them get to you. Don't argue.

Baba came out and said, 'Tomorrow, go and see Anuja. That might cheer her up.'

I didn't want to hurt him by saying an outright 'No' so I said, 'Let's see. I'll phone and go.'

When it became clear that you had left with Anuja, I began to look for reasons.

We became friends almost instantly. With me, this was a first. We both disliked girls who sang light classical and boys who wore banians with sleeves. Girls who had to be dropped home after rehearsal or any other practice session, rude rickshaw drivers, shepu bhaji in any form, group photographs at weddings, men who left the top two buttons of their shirts open, lizards, tea that has gone cold, the habit of taking the newspaper to the toilet, kissing a boy who'd just smoked a cigarette et cetera.

Another list. The things we loved: strong coffee, Matisse, Rumi, summer rain, bathing together, rice pancakes, Tom Hanks, Café Sunrise, black-and-white photographs, the first quiet moments after you get up in the morning. And on this latter list there was also a man we both loved very much: you. I had only met men like you in novels, men who lived their own idiosyncrasies.

Sometimes I got angry with you. You'd behave

as if you were some perverse actor; the poet of your own unreasonable spirit. Now that it's all over, I wonder if I could ever love anyone again.

I knew there would be comments and questions if I were to mope at home so I went to Rashmi's house or simply hung out in the tower room. I don't cry now. I don't even feel anger. When I do, I go into the tower room, memory floods back and washes the anger away.

I don't know whether to laugh or cry when Aai tells Baba that I'm this way because I miss Anuja. Now Anuja, who never shed a tear before all this, weeps all day, weeps until she's exhausted, and then goes to sleep without looking at me. They call what afflicts her depression and they're taking care of it.

Psychiatrists, pills, a change of scene, that sort of thing.

I didn't like Dali; now, like you, I do. Like you, I began to drink my Coke with a pinch of salt. Like you, I stopped bothering about ironed clothes. Like you, I sit with a dictionary while reading the papers. Like you, I sit on the compound wall after a bath.

Was that why? Because I began to behave like you?

Rashmi's bedroom wall features a photograph of the two of us. We're sitting on a garden bench, our backs to the camera, arms across each other's shoulders. I heard something, I think, and I looked back and Rashmi clicked. I'm not smiling in the picture but the happiness inside me radiates out of it. I told Rashmi to take it off the wall and keep it safe.

When Arindam's first email about the meeting came, you got ready albeit a little reluctantly.

We went on the bike, wandering through an unfamiliar part of the city. Once we came down the hill, it took us a while to make our way through the grandiose bungalows and we got late. Although I had been the prime mover of this expedition, I wasn't entirely ready for this meeting. But I liked the intellectual tone of Arindam's mail and I felt I had to go.

At the meeting, you behaved exactly as Marathi novelists of the last century tell us husbands do in sari shops.

At the door Arindam was taking down names and email addresses in a register. As he wrote mine, he asked, 'Are you okay with giving your postal address?'

'Yes,' I said and gave Rashmi's address with our names attached. Taking in the common address, Arindam looked up and said, 'Great! Are you a couple?' I looked at you but you said nothing and continued to read a brochure. So I said, 'Yes.'

Ten or twelve men were gathered in the room. That's where I first saw Ashish and Samuel. I thought Arindam, a shortish man with a way of waving his arms about to make a point, was talking sense.

Now with the aid of statistics and charts, he said we should get together, share experiences. It didn't matter how small the group was. What mattered was a beginning; we had to make a beginning.

Throughout the meeting a boy with reddish hair kept staring at you; this left me a little disconcerted.

On the way home, you said that you couldn't understand the need for collective action. I said, 'I am not a big one for talking clubs but at least we'll meet people with similar problems.'

You said, 'If it ain't broke, why fix it?'

'Meaning?'

'Let's face the problems when they come. Maybe it's because I've not lived in a family situation but I don't think I have any problems as such.'

Then you began to sing, cutting loose. As we rode over the hill outside the city, then when we were within city limits, through the sounds of traffic, you sang. The honking of the cars would mix with your voice but you sang on, tapping out a rhythm on my shoulder. When we stopped at signals, you ignored the traffic policeman, the people laughing at us from cars. When they rolled up their windows, you smiled and went on singing. You only stopped when we got home. Then you hugged me and said, 'Come up after dinner.'

Whistling, you took the stairs in four leaps and vanished into your room. I thought, at that moment, that I might have understood what you meant.

'Whatever happens, happens for the best!' That's how any domestic counselling starts in a Marathi family. Everyone in every family has an inner psychiatrist who rises to the occasion with some home-made mottos, a few lines from a Jagjit Singh ghazal. An older generation may quote Tukaram but underlying all this is the bedrock phrase: Whatever happens, happens for the best.

Anuja was taken to a real psychiatrist yesterday. When she was taken into the doctor's cabin, I came out and sat on the clinic steps. The rains had caused havoc: the gutters were thick with storm debris and city sludge. A school bus shuddered to a halt in front of me. A toddler tottered down the steps, trying to manage his school bag and water bottle. The bus pulled away. The boy looked around. No one seemed to be on hand to take him home; no mother, no elder sister. He sat down on the kerb, planted his chin on his hand and settled down to wait.

'Remember what I said about exercise?' It was the doctor and Anuja. 'Have you thought about going on a trek now that it's raining?'

Anuja was leaden-eyed and hardly there. In contrast, the psychiatrist's face was so receptive, so inviting that I wanted to go up to her and tell her everything. Then she added, 'Everything that happens, happens for the best.'

I burst out laughing. The doctor looked askance at me. When I turned away, the little boy was gone. I look at Anuja. I think about what happened to me. How could it have been for the best, any of it?

I sense the presence of other people. They're keeping me company without saying a word, without foisting themselves on to me. It's as if they've materialized suddenly, made me aware of them. They seem to be saying. 'Didn't you know? We were always here for you.'

In that wasted time between exams and results, I go to Rashmi's flat every afternoon. She has given me a key. I can shut out the world there. None of the doors or windows overlook the street. Through the afternoon, I move from chair to sofa, sofa to chair, checking what I feel. I break this rhythm for a cup of tea. I read the first four or five pages of the books she has. I watch blue films. I stand under the shower for a long time. And I wait for it to strike four.

At four, Rashmi returns. In one hand, her purse. In the other a stuffed bag: groceries, ironed clothes, and a special treat for me. A hot vada-pao perhaps. But it's her face, her smile, that brightens up the room and the evening.

Then I make tea for her and we both stand in the balcony to drink it and chat. At six thirty, on her way to the gym, she drops me home.

Once, when I was giving her a head massage,

I said, 'If I were that kind of boy, I'd have married you.' She said, 'Good grief. I don't think I would have married you. I could have lived with you for a week but after that I'd have had to return to my place here.' Then she rumpled my hair and said, 'That's life: the guy I could really be friends with wants nothing to do with my kind.'

Rashmi's ways are her own. I didn't talk much about you; when I did, she changed the subject. So I made a conscious effort and stopped; and you vanished from our conversations. This made me aware of something else: of how friendship can offer surcease from noise.

At six thirty, on her way back to the gym, Rashmi drops me home. Aseem was still at the office; the parents were at Sharayu Maushi's home. I unlock the gate, then the front door, go in. At Rashmi's, it's possible to close a single door and lock out the world. In our home, even after you've closed the front door behind you, the world has many ways of sneaking back in. There's the back door, the side entrance. Facing the road, four windows. Five at the back. Many of the rooms don't have doors, just thresholds. No one can be alone here. Any number of people can be watching you at any given time: family, neighbours, the vegetable vendors passing by. Each of us must perform our joys and sorrows for all the rest because this house has a front door, a back door and a side entrance. And often, no doors between rooms.

On the door of a cupboard, you had stuck the photograph of your parents—who you had lost in an air crash. You didn't say much about them. I never saw you perform any of the rituals of ancestor worship. Your father had been a consultant to the Indian embassy in Paris; your mother a journalist. The French language flowed through your family, as the Hanuman stotra and the verses of Sant Ramdas did in other families. In their five-year Paris stint, they took you there, but only once. Your memories as an eight-year-old: the Eiffel tower by night, sunlight until eight in the evening, and a variety of exciting cheeses.

Perhaps it was because your father had always been abroad, but you spoke a little more about your mother. I liked listening to you talk about her.

You remembered her sitting at a table, spectacles perched on the top of her head, writing. As someone who put you into a papoose and took you to the market. As someone who munched popcorn with you as you watched English movies together.

When your father returned and took your mother's attention from you, you resented it. In your box of books, there were often two copies of the same novel, one with your father's name and one with your mother's.

My mother has no cupboard of her own. Alone at home as a child, I would investigate the secrets of each cupboard. One day, I chose the kitchen cupboard. I found a list of Aai's medicines, a bunch of Sharayu Maushi's letters written from Sangli, a few five-rupee and ten-rupee notes, a recipe for eggless cake torn from a magazine, a postal savings book . . . all redolent of naphthalene balls.

When I saw that your parents' photograph was missing from the cupboard, I knew for certain that you weren't going to return.

What did I know about your family? Your parents, that lawyer Mr Dixit who was in charge of your inheritance, your Seema Maushi who took you into her home for her own selfish motives, her perverted husband who made a plaything of your body when you were too innocent to know what was going on.

Then it occurs to me, you got no letters. If there were phone calls, they were from friends you'd made after coming to the city. No question about email, you didn't like email.

What happened to everyone else? College friends? Distant relatives? School buddies? A schoolteacher, even? An old family retainer? No one? What did you do with them?

What did you think you'd do to me?

You listened with empathy, with attentiveness. In the night, you'd help Abbas down the shutter and upend the chairs. You'd listen to him rant about the rising price of potatoes, the changes in customer behaviour, the difficulties his nephew was facing in America after September 11. You'd give Abbas your undivided attention, listening with your eyes, smiling, encouraging him to speak.

And no doubt, he would feel that it was all worthwhile, because there was someone at the end of the day, someone to listen and to smile.

I can't remember you ever sitting down to talk to Baba or Aseem like that. But from time to time, you'd chat with Aai. One day, I came home from college to find the door ajar and no one inside the house. I followed the sound of voices into the backyard. Through the kitchen window, I could see Aai weeding with a trowel and you holding a bunch of curry leaves. Aai was talking away, words running on, ideas flowing into each other.

That night, I asked you, 'Were you really paying attention? Or was that your listening face?' You did not answer. Instead, you recounted how

Malti Aatya had been cured of rheumatism thanks to a godman's prasad; how Anuja and I had no religion left in us; of the two young women Aseem had checked out as prospective brides. You told me how coriander and chillies had to be planted separately, how oddly Tulsi was behaving in the night-time soap, and then you added, 'It's not just my ears but my mind that is engaged as well. In a couple of years, your name will be added to the list in the marriage bureau. So be ready.'

I had no idea how to get ready. I was sure that your parents would have told you about such matters. Mine would rather die.

I had often wanted to say to Arindam: you can't just go back into history to collect proof. You have to find evidence from ancient times that we're normal. If you can't find references to our kind in the Ramayana, the Mahabharata or the Bible, who's going to listen to us? At least, we could ask why Lakshmana had felt the need to leave his wife and children behind and follow Rama into the wilderness.

One rainy night, you were listening to me and Arindam talking. Your back was wet with the rain coming through the open window. A few drops fell into the beer mugs too. The drumming of the rain on the roof was loud enough for me to have to tell Arindam to speak up a bit.

'Every important political change has happened because of a movement. That's the critical element, Tanay. We have to organize. We have to fight injustice constitutionally,' he said with the fervour of a revolutionary.

'But what would this movement's agenda be? Our own independent newspapers, our pubs, our theatre, our this, our that? We can't make a break from the rest of the world and demand equality on our own terms. We don't seem different in any way from the Establishment.'

I was weighing my words as I spoke but it was clear that Arindam wasn't getting it. He kept trying to interrupt but I kept raising my voice and pressing on with what I was saying. I looked at you, you raised your eyebrows, quietly amused. But your face also showed pride in my stance.

And I thought, at least I'm getting through to somebody. I came and sat by you. The rain wet my back too.

It was only when the rain stopped and the smell of the raat rani came pouring into the room that Arindam got up to leave. He shook your hand and said, 'You don't talk much?' You just laughed. I knew that Arindam would take your silence to mean consent. Aai, wiping her hands on her sari, would look at you, sitting there with the curry leaves in your hand and think, 'He's so much better than my son. At least he doesn't argue.' Abbas would think whatever the problems he was confronted with, at least there was someone to listen, to smile, and he would be calmed.

As usual, the police handed over the city to the goons, for a period of ten days. Aseem was late returning from work. Baba was afraid that the crowds would swell and so he put the idol into its salver and carried it into every room of the house. Earlier, he would go into the tower room as well. This time he didn't. Every year he went barefoot to the immersion; this time, he put on his slippers. I carried a dabba in which there were slices of banana meant for general distribution. Aai brought up the rear with a bag in which there were two faces of Gauri, a stone representing the virgin goddess Hartalika and the flowers that had been offered to the deity and then discarded. As we walked away, my father turned around thrice to show the idol our home.

The ghat had been lit with halogen lamps for the immersion. Little aartis were being performed on either side of the steps. Baba gave the idol to a couple of damp young men whose bodies smelled of moss. We watched as they bore him off.

As we were climbing the steps, Nadkarni Kaka was bringing his Ganpati down for immersion. With him was Nadkarni Kaku, their three daughters and sixteen girls from the hostel. They were singing filmi aartis. I left the parents with them and came home, picking my way through the dirt and the crowds.

The house was quiet. The previous days had turned it into a bazaar with women, aartis, noise, offerings, haldi-kunku, all competing for attention. Now that the immersion had happened, the house seemed to sigh with relief. I decided that it was the last time I would go to immerse the idol. Aai and Baba could do it themselves, if they wished.

As soon as I got back, Anuja fled on the bike. I began to climb the stairs to the tower room. It seemed still and quiet too. A golden light filtered through the windows and on to the terrace. A thumri by Iqbal Bano floated in the air. Everything seemed to be in its place. The rolls of canvas, the CDs in their racks, the photographs on the wall. In the middle of the room, there was an earthen bowl filled with kevda flowers. I heard the sound of the shower and then it was turned off. You came out of the bathroom, a towel wrapped around your hips, your hair wet. You smiled and your lips, still moist from the shower, seemed cold to me. I remained where I was, in a chair in the corner. You sat down on a mat and began to cut your toenails with great care. Then you anointed yourself with a sweet-smelling moisturizer. You took out an ironed shirt and a crisp pair of shorts and laid them out on the bed. You took off the towel and threw it in the direction of the bathroom, from which the last wisps of steam were still escaping.

You took a fresh canvas and placed it on the easel. You selected a brush. Then you turned to the bed and put on the clothes. Next, the curtains at the window facing the ladies' hostel—you drew them back. Then you sat down quietly in front of me.

You had nowhere to go. No one was coming to see you. And I had watched this ritual sringara as if it had been a short film, made specially for me. I could not remember a time when I had paid such attention to my own body.

You got up and came to sit by me, bringing a bouquet of aromas with you. I wanted nothing more than to have you sit by me. After a while, you got up, picked up the brush and incised the canvas with a single blue streak. Then you came and laid your head in my lap and fell into a deep sleep.

Now that the rains were over, Baba wanted to clean up the gutters on the roof. He was going to climb a ladder and he needed me to hold it in place. And as I stood there, I heard Rashmi's car come to a halt outside the house. She took a box out of the back of the car and walked purposefully into the house. Before I could call out or say anything, she began to climb the stairs to the tower room. I called her name, loud enough to get past the headphones on her ears, but she paid me no heed. Baba called out a warning; he didn't want my attention wandering from the task at hand.

Rashmi had been wanting to meet you. She waited for me to introduce us but in vain. 'One day, I'll just show up and meet him,' she warned me. That you should show a similar interest in meeting someone seemed impossible; but you were both the kind who did as you pleased.

For the longest time, I had wondered if I should tell Rashmi about us. I couldn't even persuade myself that what we had was really happening so how could I tell anyone else about it? Sometimes, I'd find the words hovering on my lips when I was strolling around the campus with her. Or when she asked questions like, 'Why do you wear these crumpled clothes?' or 'Why do you always have to run home?' or 'There's a secret smile playing around your lips. What's up?' Once, without warning, I put my head in her lap and said that I knew that she knew that I had something I wanted to tell her. She said, 'Whatever.'

Finally it happened without premeditation. One day, I got to rehearsals early. The College Recreation Hall was empty and I sprawled on a bench waiting for everyone to show up. And then I realized I could smell you on my body. I got up, went to the library, called Rashmi out and told her everything, as we stood together at the door.

The ground was too slippery for me to let go of the ladder and run after Rashmi. She shouldn't have gone up without a warning. Who knew what state you might be in?

'Rashmi's here,' I said to Baba, but his mind was in the gutters and his only concern was to sprinkle me with dirty water. He heard nothing and, for the next fifteen minutes, I kept twisting my neck to peer up at the tower room. And then, at last, Baba came down the ladder. He got to the last step and said, 'Dash it, I've left the stick broom up there.'

'Never mind,' I said. 'You use it only to clean those gutters.'

'No, no, hold on tight.'

When he was finally done, I raced up the stairs, taking them two at a time. I could hear both of you laughing.

At least you were fully dressed.

When you got your board exam results, the school was full of parents and children.

Uncomfortable, you slipped away. You were the only one who had come alone to get his results. For the next six or seven months, you were always close to tears, tears that would not fall.

You began what you described as your accomplished solitude from that day. This term—accomplished solitude—struck me deeply. And it slowly began to dawn on you that you did not need people around you when you were painting or reading, when you were watching a film with deep concentration, or when you sat down to eat, chewing every mouthful and savouring every flavour. You made loneliness easy on yourself.

When you took your results and got to Seema Maushi's home, the door was locked. Bruno was lolling in the backyard. He began to bark at you. Frightened, you sat down on the staircase and waited, baking in the sun.

'If you were locked in a room, without books, without paper or pen, okay, without electricity too, what would you do?' I asked you once.

'Why a day? A week. A month. I'd just sit there, happy.'

Your feet were red from the burning stone when Seema Maushi's husband returned in his jeep. Inside the house, he hugged you, praised your performance and let his hands wander all over your body. This had been going on for a couple of months. When you felt his weight on your body one night, you tried to scream. He grabbed your mouth and stifled your screams.

You would wake up screaming, sometimes. When I tried to take you into my arms to comfort you, you would push me away and withdraw into a corner, seeking solitude.

He had not even cared enough to protect your certificate from crumpling by putting it into a file. After an hour, he left and Seema Maushi returned. You sat her down and told her what her husband was. You showed her what he had done to your body and then you packed your bag and went off to Mr Dixit, the lawyer. Then began a saga of college hostels and rented rooms. After you finished the twelfth standard, you asked Mr Dixit to sell the Mumbai flat, the shares, the three cars and the land near Kolhapur.

Until your paintings began to sell, you would have enough to live on.

A bunch of us had gone to see a film. We had booked an entire row and occupied it, chattering and giggling. Next to me sat Monica whose mobile rang incessantly. Only the day before I had announced that we were to have a paying guest. And then Monica began to shriek. She pointed to a man in the audience and we began to laugh. He was wearing a clean white dhotar and red mulmul sadra, chappals on his feet. He had come to see the film. Alone. The man was you.

'You went to see a film?' I asked you that evening. 'Alone?'

For the next two years, through your first two years of college, the bitterness had not abated. Everything around you seemed odd and false. All relationships seemed temporary.

In junior college, you had no friends. In your free time, your pursuits were solitary. You would sit in your hostel room reading for hours. Or you would go for long jogs; or have a meal alone in a restaurant. On Sunday, you'd climb a hill and paint. Or play the guitar.

To put on clothes dictated only by what you felt like wearing and to go out and see a film alone was therefore no novelty. I can't do that. Even today, I need company to see a film, to look at paintings, to celebrate, even to read. For if I can't talk about the film's plot or the book's nuances to someone, if I can't listen to what they're saying, what's the point?

You're so set in your ways, so clear about your decisions, will you ever notice that it isn't necessary to be so cut and dried about everything?

Every Sunday, you would empty out the tower room. Then you'd walk about, hand on chin, looking at it. Then you'd bring each thing in again and set it down in a different place.

This relooking business infected me as well. I began to look at, to really look at, things: at leaves and at the sky, at boiled milk and at your palette, at cobwebs. Van Gogh showed me an overheated sky. Husain raced thoroughbreds at me, Seurat drew pointillist rangolis in my head, Picasso showed me many simultaneous aspects of the human face, Dali melted time for me and mysterious Anjolie Ela Menon . . .

You had a way of looking at things which seemed sharp, perceptive, cobalt blue. But when I turned my gaze on my folks, on my home, a disquiet was born inside me. With the disquiet came the questions.

In the hall, a man-sized showcase. Here a speaker, there a speaker. Here an elephant, there an elephant. A plastic flowerpot. The grocery store's free calendar, cups of an intensely floral design, Aseem's tie, a photograph of my grandparents. If all these things were to be ground together, the result would be the indeterminate green of a fungus.

In a crumpled fig-coloured T-shirt and blue jeans, you once said to me: 'Forget about symmetry, Tanay; forget about balance.' When I complained that I had no room of my own, you said, 'This Sunday, redo the tower room. Make it yours.' I felt a warm russet glow behind my eyes.

That Sunday when you went to Sunrise for breakfast, I began to empty the room.

When I told Rashmi about you, she said to me, 'All of us have to give shape to our lives, Tanay. You have to choose your own design. You have to keep changing it, working with it. You have to shape your taste as well. And that means trusting what pleases you.'

It took me about forty-five minutes to finish. I liked what I had done to the room. I admired it from different standpoints. I sat down and waited. I waited until noon but still you did not come.

At one o'clock you came back carrying a sketch of Mehnaz. I was sitting on the staircase, bored, hungry, angry.

At Sunrise, you looked up and saw Mehnaz combing her hair in the window. After breakfast, you went up to ask if she would sit for you. When she agreed, you forgot about me and my version of a room of my own.

I could tell how proud you were of the sketch you were showing me. We were both intent on enjoying what we had done. After about half an hour in the room, you realized that I had changed the room around. I was rewarded with a look of approval.

Such colours, such colours. When you breathe out, I see red and yellow flashes in front of my eyes. When we're in the bath together, surrounded by a surfeit of steam, it's a misty blue. When the sun is shining and we look at each other from a distance, and we smile, it's white, a shining white. If I'm talking to someone and mention you, my face changes, it's a dark blue. Dark brown when I call out to you; peaceful green when you call out to me.

How could anyone believe that you did not love me? Right up to the time you left, you did not change the way I had organized the room.

At the meeting, Arindam looked up from the register and a real smile burst across his face. 'Alone?' he asked, looking past my shoulder. I shrugged.

There were some newcomers at the meeting.
Samuel was also alone, who knew why? The
chair next to him seemed symbolically vacant,
but that might have been because I was feeling
lonely. The people around me seemed a little
strange; again, I had not felt this way at the first
meeting.

Arindam began the proceedings by reading a
story. It was set in a port and it was about a love
affair between the son of the owner of a ship
and a poor worker on board the ship. Forty
years later, Christmas night, New York, crowded
pub, young man sees poor worker drunk and
desolate . . . something like that. No one was
really paying attention to the story, which
described, and quite beautifully too, what might
go on in your mind if you were suddenly
presented with a living embodiment of your
past. After the story was done, the newcomers
were introduced to the group.

It seemed as if a whole platoon of gym-toned
bodies had descended on the spot. Many of
them were sporting rings in their left ears. I

remembered some of them from the station road. I was amazed at Arindam's diligence. There was to be a conference in Mumbai. There were obstacles to be surmounted, permissions to be sought, an antagonistic press and the usual bunch of Sanatan dharmi right-wingers to be dealt with. Arindam began to talk about our rights. He was to be a delegate at the conference. He wanted to be briefed on the issues. The conference website was to be inaugurated ... Two young men who had been eyeing each other made their way out together.

'Do you think it will be all conferences and talks in Mumbai?' I asked Samuel.

'Do you want to go with Arindam?' he asked.

I was quite surprised when you agreed to go. Had you not been there, I would have felt quite lonely. But when you were there, I kept worrying about their unsubtle advances. That was the first and last party we attended. Dancing to loud music wasn't something new; I quite enjoyed it. Powered by beer, we danced until our legs were aching, our bodies soaked with sweat despite the air conditioning. I went to the counter, bought myself a beer, and began to watch you dancing alone. For a while, I seemed to go deaf. The multicoloured lights began to merge into one. And suddenly, nothing seemed clear. Who are you? Would you acknowledge me if I met you on the street in broad daylight? What do you want? What is going to happen after this? My head began to spin.

Around us, a sea of men. In shorts and tight banians. In jeans and T-shirts that showed the bodies they had earned in the gym. Married men with paunches packed into full-sleeved shirts. A flamboyant drag queen with a face of stone. All of them were dancing as if no one was watching. It was a near-orgy. The men were draped across each other, at the tables in the corners.

What did I want? What did Arindam think he would achieve? At one of the tables in a corner, Ashish and Samuel were nursing their drinks and a quiet conversation. I put my drink down on the table and went up to you. I did up all the buttons on your shirt and said, 'Let's go.'

You followed me out immediately. Only when we were back in the tower room and I had wrapped my arms around you did I feel safe again.

Manjiri's kelvan. All Baba's relatives arrived to stay. Durga Aji had brought a year's supply of sesame chutney and papads. Sita Kaku and Kanchan had put on weight. Since Arjun had just begun to walk, his mother Kanchan and everyone else seemed to spend much of their time chasing him about. Anuja took Prachi for a haircut and the loss of those long, lustrous locks sent Durga Aji into a rage that came and went over the next two days.

Prakash Kaka looked a little tired. After dinner, he and Ram Kaka and Baba would go for a paan and a walk. The house was busy, vibrant, a fairground. The pleasure of so many guests kept Aai in a state of constant ferment. Even Aseem had taken four days' leave. Every evening, there were party games and until the last boiled peanut had been eaten it was impossible to even think of coming upstairs. Durga Aji was measuring Aseem and Sunil for wedding shervanis in her head, even as she cracked her knuckles meditatively. After dinner, sitting on a cot and watching these people, I thought: I rather like them. I felt soft and warm and welcoming. Manjiri said, 'Now that I'm going far away to Nagpur, we're not going to see much of each other. You'd better keep in touch on email.'

I looked up at that moment and saw you with an armful of wet clothes. I felt ashamed that I hadn't been to see you for two whole days. I came up and looked down; the afternoon sunlight flattened my family into dwarfs.

Six months after you vanished, in the middle of a storm of beating rain and theatrical thunder, Anuja returned. The storm had given us no warning and so Aai had sent me to close all the doors and windows, thus plunging the house into darkness. After Anuja's departure, Aai had begun to look like she was slowly falling apart; in this gloom, she looked even stranger. Baba dug out a sweater and put on his slippers and slumped into an armchair. I was channel surfing mindlessly.

Aseem came back from the office and Aai made tea. As he was tossing his smelly socks into the bathroom, the bell rang. He went to the door, carrying with him the smell of his feet. He opened it and shouted, 'Aai-Baba.' We were all electrified. And there she was. Anuja, who had returned as she had left, with no warning. She looked as if she hadn't slept for days. Her hands seemed thin. Her hair was a little longer. Her clothes seemed old and torn. No, she was wearing your clothes. So your clothes seemed old and torn. Your torn clothes stifled all my responses.

While I was conducting this examination, she was weeping in Aai's embrace. I looked at her and managed a smile. Until then, I had laboured under the impression that you and she had left in different directions.

I went into my room and watched the rain. Moisture had seeped through the wall and the photographs were all crooked now. My illusions stripped from me, I felt my body go hot. I felt a sense of loss; the world felt a deceitful place.

No one could talk to her that day. She had a bath, a hot meal and then slept for twenty-four hours at a stretch. By then, the light was back in the house and questions were on every face. Anuja woke up and began to cry again. She begged Aai-Baba's forgiveness. Sharayu Maushi and Nadkarni Kaku turned up to give Aai moral support. Baba went to inform the police. Anuja refused to tell the police anything.

When Anuja began to talk, when it was all put into words, I felt no anger, just misery, aridity.

In the evening, when I was sitting in the tower room, doing nothing, Anuja came upstairs and peered in. She was in the mood to talk. She told me that you had left her, without warning, suddenly, one morning. I could offer no consolation. But as we came down the stairs, I wanted to drag her back up and throw her off the roof.

In the next few days, my mind was a desert. Just as it was when you vanished. No, I should face it. Just as it was when you ran away with Anuja. I wasn't shocked then. Nor did I feel any anger. I had decided that I would wait for you. When you didn't show up all day, I ran to Sunrise. Menden said that you hadn't even come for breakfast. The next day, when I asked whether you had said anything about travelling, Mehnaz said you had paid your bill a day earlier. The photograph of your parents was missing too. When Baba ransacked the tower room, I found some photographs, other ones. I began my vigil.

Two days after Anuja returned, she was sent to a psychiatrist. She was sent to live with Sharayu Maushi for a change of scene. Rashmi took me into her care and managed to bring me back to my senses.

I've had many people come and go in my life. I didn't see myself as having been cheated by anyone. This time everything was different. This time changed every tomorrow.

I have no tears now. Why should I? No one

around me would understand. But memory surges back, hot and fresh. In your arms a stack of books. Your favourites. The image is out of focus now so I can't make out the titles. And your face, above the books, filled with laughter. Behind it the fuzzy light that spilled from the room.

Another photo I found in the debris of Baba's room raid.

Anuja

10 July

Today, I told Dr Khanvilkar that I seem to have made only bad decisions. My life was not the way I wanted it to be. I told her that I thought I was going to have to live one of those fraudulent lives I saw around me.

To which she said, 'Are you the only one who wants to live differently? Those who choose to live differently must suffer the consequences. They must take the pain their decisions bring. Anyway, you're still young. Why should you accept defeat?'

I wonder if I should believe what she says. But when you're not strong in yourself, anyone can tell you anything and you'll fall for it.

Today, I also looked at myself in the mirror: swollen face, dark circles under sunken eyes, white tongue, hair like nylon to the touch. My face tells of the side effects of the drugs they're giving me.

At that moment, I wanted to end it all. I did not feel I could go on. I went into Sharayu Maushi's bathroom and opened a bottle of eau de cologne and drank as much as I could in a single gulp. My mouth and throat began to burn; I dropped the bottle which fell and broke. I couldn't even swallow; it came out again. This was failure piled on failure and I sat down in the middle of the glass and the intense smell and began to wail. Sharayu Maushi and Aai came running to see what was going on. Aai took in the broken bottle and began to rain blows down on me. I gritted my teeth and took her blows. Sharayu Maushi interposed herself. Aai tried to push her away and said, 'You want to die? If we can hurt you so much, why did you come back? Go now, find some other man and elope with him.'

Then she began to weep. My leaving must have hit her hard. I think she needs a psychiatrist more than I do.

But her weeping caused a fresh storm inside my head. I thumped off into the hall and put on the television. A woman was singing a bhajan. I raised the volume until it drowned out the world and locked the door and sat there, barely listening. I did not open the door until Baba came in the evening. He gave me a lecture about my duties. Aai decided that we would stay in Sharayu Maushi's house for a week. My sentence begins tomorrow morning. I told Baba, 'Don't worry. I'm not about to commit suicide. I don't have that kind of courage. If I did, would I have come back?'

He listened, his face like stone, like cold stone.

'Right,' he said and then added: 'Until the time you get married, you will behave yourself according to the house rules. You will obey. We gave you your freedom and we saw what you did with it.'

I slapped my forehead and walked off.

My finger had been hurting since the afternoon. When I looked at it carefully, I saw a sliver of glass embedded in the skin. I took a needle and slowly, carefully, drew it out.

12 July

Dr Khanvilkar suggested that I write a diary. Why is she so interested in my life? Because she's being paid to be interested, right? Otherwise why would she tolerate me sitting there, my face contorted, blabbering away for an hour, every other day? If my parents sat there instead of Dr K, they might learn something about me and we'd save a lot of money. But they don't want to hear any of this. They want it wrapped up, put away, forgotten. As you might take a car to the garage, I was brought to Sharayu Maushi's house. To be repaired.

I'm not sure I can write every day. I told Dr K that. I also told her that I wasn't about to share what I wrote with her. To which she said in a honeysweet voice, the kind you hear those announcers use on the radio, 'Write whatever comes to your mind. What you feel now. What you felt then. It doesn't matter if you don't write every day.' I wasn't paying much attention.

Thinking brings more questions to the surface. My head begins to hurt because no one has any convincing answers. Why did this happen to me? And when everything was going so well, why did he vanish? Did I do something wrong? Or did he feel nothing for me?

They've sent me here, far away from home, to Sharayu Maushi's house. For a change of scene, they say. She and Aai are going to keep an eye on me. I hate it here. They behave as if I'm some kind of mental patient. And then, it's an odd place: far from the city, no trees, no gardens, just an expanse of plots and half-built bungalows. The house bakes in the afternoon sun. I toss and turn, wondering if it's a frying pan I'm lying on. I don't look out of the window. It's supposed to be the monsoons but the sky is clear. My head swims. Aai sits with Sharayu Maushi, crying over spilt milk. I'm tired of crying. When I finished school, I thought I had grown up, I thought I had become independent. I felt I could stand on my own feet. Now I'm a child again, a helpless child.

When I realized he was gone and I decided to come home to my mother, nothing was clear. In a trance, I packed. Half the clothes were his. As were those on my body. I set out to burn those clothes when Sharayu Maushi stopped me and took them away for the gardener's son. The result? Those very clothes kept crossing my line of vision. I complained to Sharayu Maushi who gave the boy a month's leave.

Tanay has changed. The other day, he acted very strange. He said he had come to see me but most of the time he just sat there, saying nothing. Then he went to the cupboard, opened my bag and took out the olive-green T-shirt and left. Like the gardener's son, he's going to be wandering about in those clothes too.

They punish me with their silences. I keep telling the doctor this.

One morning, I woke up and looked around

to find him missing. He hadn't returned even after I'd made myself some tea. Afternoon came but he didn't. His cycle was gone too. I shoved my feet into slippers and went to look for him. The library, I thought. No. The seashore? No. The streets? Nowhere. By evening, I began to feel lonely. Had he left a letter? I tumbled everything out of the cupboard. His bag was gone. Also some of his clothes. Other things too. That's when it hit me: he had left me. I had not eaten, I began to feel dizzy. I found that I had two hundred rupees in my pocket. In one of his trouser pockets, I found another fifty-rupee note. I had dinner and returned to sit on the steps with the door open.

Nothing.

Next day. Nothing.

I began to get frightened. There had been nothing to warn me. In the past few days, he had taken to sleeping on the floor alone but we had not fought or anything like that. I asked the few acquaintances we had made if they had seen him. I described him to those we did not know. Such a small town but no one had seen him. In the evening when I returned to the room, I began to feel dizzy again. I did not have the nerve to tell the police. I tried instead to figure out what had happened.

Bag? Gone.

Personal stuff? Gone.

Clothes hanging on the wall? Gone.

Had he planned this? What was I to do?

Finally, I got up and packed. The rent for the next two months had already been paid but that didn't matter. I didn't know where to go. I hadn't much money left. As I put on my shoes, I realized I would have to go home to my parents. Where else?

I sat down to think about it. It took me all day. Where could he have gone? Would he return? I kept looking for reasons. I tried to remember exactly what he had said, the precise words he had used in the days before his departure. But I could find no clue to his behaviour.

I had never spent so much time thinking about someone else. I hadn't even thought about an issue in this sustained way. I was impulsive; if I felt like it, I would do it. I had once been a climber. In the heat of the afternoon, I would drag myself up narrow footpaths to the top of a hill. Keeping fear at bay, I would scramble up steep hillsides, often with the help of ropes. When the group arrived at the top, huffing and puffing, everyone would take a breather and stop to admire the view. Not me. I would walk to the very edge of the summit and look down as the wind screamed around my ears.

From there, the villages and fields look like they belong in a picture, the jagged edges of the mountain framing a burning sun. Then I would suddenly be filled with a great joy and my mind would say, 'You want to. You know you do. What is there to hold you back? Jump. What you feel now, what you want now, that's all there is. Jump. Just jump.'

13 July

If truth be told, Aai and Baba should not have felt so bad about my going away with him. I had done it before, left, I mean. Usually, I would tell them and go. This time I had not told anyone and left. That was the only difference. Otherwise, I had always planned on leaving.

How long could I have stayed in this world of Aai's religion and her swamis, her rituals and fasts; this world of Baba's, he who was always afraid of what 'they' would say; this world of marriage and children and aunts who performed the Mangala Gauri ritual to signify their happiness with their married state, and cousins who organized rose-giving competitions on Valentine's Day? I messed up my first escape attempt. I wonder if there's something wrong with me.

For the first time, Aai took some time to try and talk to me and be my friend. What she wanted to tell me, I had learned from books and from the conversations and experiences of my friends. I listened, keeping my face blank. I wonder why she had never tried this before. The strange thing is that she never tried to do the same thing again. It was a game she played with me for a single day. She was ashamed and she wanted to hide her shame. Once you try something hypocritical, you can never sound convincing again.

Until yesterday, I thought I was feeling better. But in the afternoon, my limbs began to feel heavy and I felt alone again. The future frightened me so much I began to cry. I did not know what was going to happen to me. I felt that everyone must be laughing at me. My head began to fuzz over. Sitting in a chair, I began to cry copiously. I wept on and on until my breath began to catch in my throat. Then I went and locked myself in my room and continued to cry. Sharayu Maushi realized something was wrong;

she began to bang on the door. I didn't move. She went on banging for half an hour. I grew tired, physically tired of crying. It was only when poor Sharayu Maushi climbed a ladder to peer in at the window that I got up and opened the door. She gave me some pills and put me to bed and drew a sheet over me. I stuffed a handkerchief into my mouth to stifle my sobs.

I remember his mood, the day we left home together. He didn't seem excited or anything. I said, 'Hey, let's get this straight. I'm the one who's leaving home. But you're the one with the long face.' When I went up to his room with my haversack, his paints and brushes were packed, his canvases rolled up. When I knocked, it took him a while to open the door. I remained standing on the staircase. I felt sure that Baba would not go to the police for fear of a scandal. After a trek to Mudumalai with our ecobuddies, he was going to take me to Pondicherry. And after that? Neither of us knew. Finally he came out. He didn't lock the door.

I didn't look back but he kept turning around

to catch a glimpse of his room. At around three, we left the city on the general compartment of a train, crowded in with hundreds of other people. At the campsite, he kept drawing that room, again and again.

Returning from the doctor, I told Aai to tell the rickshaw driver to take us via the college. (These days, I have only to ask.) When college came into view, I felt a great sadness. I had dropped out. I had lost a year. I saw Neha and Amrita going in. I thought of calling out to them. Anubhav's Honda was in the parking lot. Had he found someone else?

I should call them all, one by one.

I poked my head out of the rickshaw. On both sides of the road, huge hoardings. On the hoardings, huge faces. On the faces, huge smiles. Day and night, rain and sun, they would smile and smile and smile. Their monstrous faces seemed to be mocking the little people, the real people, who walked beneath them. Soft drinks, newspapers, petrol, television serials, soap: every billboard had the same huge smooth faces. I drew my head back into the rickshaw.

Today, the phone rang four times in the afternoon. When I picked it up, no one answered. I shouted 'Hello, hello,' but the person hung up. It rang again immediately. I picked up the phone and ran out to the terrace. In a soft voice, I said, 'It's me, Anuja. Talk to me. Where are you? No problems, no? Come and see me soon.' Once again, he hung up.

The third and fourth time, silence. I was waiting for the calls, standing on the terrace, my gaze anxious and unseeing. Then it stopped. No more calls. The floor began to singe my feet. I walked into the house and the darkness swamped me. I felt the house swing about my head. I couldn't see anything. I waited it out, holding on to the back of a chair. Then, with hesitant steps, I went to my room and dropped on to the bed.

Once I had gone to Rajgad in the wee hours of the morning and come back by rickshaw. The driver didn't have change so I shouted to Aai and picked up my haversack. That's when he turned up with two ten-rupee notes in his hand.

'I'm the new paying guest,' he said, 'if you don't mind . . .'

'You've just proved you're the paying guest,' I said.

He probably didn't get the joke but then few people get my jokes. He looked bemused. I thanked him and shook his hand and I might have even hurt his delicate fingers. I went into the house. I had registered that the new paying guest was a good-looking fellow but his hand was cold. Like grabbing some veggies from the fridge.

I didn't see him for the next couple of days. One morning, I was eating pohe when the phone rang. 'Call him,' Aai said. I was about to go upstairs when she said, 'Call him from the courtyard. No need to go up.'

When he disconnected, Aai invited him to sample her pohe. He sat down and applied himself to the food. He didn't know me at all then so we didn't talk.

One day, Tanay was washing the bike in the courtyard. I was in the house getting the mud

off my canvas shoes. I heard him shouting,
'One of you must be looking for this.' I looked
out of the window and gasped. He was waving
my bra at the Nadkarni Girls' Hostel as he
shouted. He was only wearing a pair of shorts.
Tanay dropped the bucket and came into the
house. A dead silence took hold of the Nadkarni
Girls' Hostel. He hooked the bra to the clothes
line and went off.

I went out and took the bra off the line and
marched up to where he was sitting on the wall.
He was listening to his Walkman, his eyes closed.
I batted him a good one. He opened his eyes.
When he saw the bra in my hand, he took the
earphones out of his ears. With my hands on
my hips, I said, 'Mine. You got a problem with
that?' He slitted his eyes and grinned.

Dr Khanvilkar said, 'If you get hyper when
you're writing, close your eyes, take deep breaths
and then look at each memory carefully and try
to discard it. Examine it, see it for what it is,
throw it away.'

14 July

I told Dr K, 'Memories of him. All memories of him.'

Dr K said, 'If the memories don't hurt too much, let them come. Don't bottle them up. Everything will clear up eventually.'

My attention strayed to her desk. On the far edge there was a glass frame with a family photograph. At the very corner. A slight push would send it over the edge. My fingers kept wandering there. I thought: I should just tell her and then pick it up and smash it.

When he took over the upstairs room, Aai-Baba declared it a no-go area for me. After the bra incident, he began to warm up. Once, after Aai had shouted herself hoarse, I was washing my hair and drying it vigorously. Through the towel, I could hear someone strumming a guitar.

First it was only random notes, plink plonk plink. My room was right under his. I came into the middle room and settled down to listen. A minute of silence; then a tune, played fluently, effortlessly. And then his voice, joining in. 'Your Song' by Elton John. I ran upstairs. My childhood dream had been that someone should play the guitar and I would sing along, even in my rough deep voice. I opened the door quietly and went in. He saw me but he didn't stop playing. Involuntarily, I started to sing. In my untrained, anyoldhow voice.

Everything stopped when Baba began to look for me, calling my name. I sat still until he gave up. I looked around and realized he had changed everything in the upstairs room. It had been bare, like something out of Gandhiji's ashram. Now everything was painted. There were mats on the floor, a mattress, books and CDs in a basket . . . crazy. And it also occurred to me that I was sitting very close to him. But I figured that

I liked it and I just kept sitting that way. Eventually, he got up and made coffee. He showed me some of his paintings; most of them seemed abstract and boring. But through all this, he neglected one well-known rule of conduct. That when a woman comes into your room, and you're wearing only shorts, you should at least put on a shirt. I rather liked that.

Neha and Anubhav came to meet me. With his new mustachios, Anubhav looks like a responsible and serious young man. Or do they all put on this look for me? It was good to meet Neha though. 'You'd better come back to college, okay? If you want company, I'll also drop out this year. I'm so glad you're back; I was getting really bored.' Anubhav was amused and uncomfortable that he was amused. I think he wanted to talk to me on his own. He seemed like someone who had experienced great pain. I couldn't meet his eyes. We both knew what had been going on. Anubhav had been my classmate since fifth standard; and he knows me better than anyone should know another person. Which is why he also knows that right now I am in no mood to offer any explanations.

When we were in Class Nine, everyone paired off. These pairs would last until about the eleventh standard. Nothing like that was going to happen to me, of that I was certain. I spent no time in front of the mirror. My voice was rough, my shoes were coated with mud, I had no time for jewellery. All I had in my favour was my fair Konkanastha complexion.

Perhaps as a result, I have always found a tawny complexion attractive. I tried to get a tan by roaming about in the sun. Meanwhile, the others in my class were exchanging greeting cards, the girls were swathing themselves against the sun, and riding side-saddle on the boys' bikes on prim excursions to Sinhagadh or the cinema. I was up for none of this. Of this, I was certain. I had so few social skills that once, when we went to have lunch at Amala's house, I fell asleep right after the meal and began to snore.

After the tenth standard board exams, we went hiking to Nepal. At Jalpaiguri, we met a bunch of Green Earth volunteers. I had been meaning to look for a summer job. I had offered to help at a snake farm but there had been no reply. So I decided I'd volunteer with Green Earth. I filled out a form; Anubhav filled one out too. Why? I hadn't bothered to ask. But on the trek, I noticed that he had begun to do as I did. But then what other models did he have? He was the kind who wore checked shirts tucked into trousers that had two demure pleats in the front.

Tanned from the trek, we came back and went to the local Green Earth office. I met some interesting folks there; the vacations were going to be exciting.

The work was easy. All over the world Green Earth needed money and volunteers who would help them raise funds and awareness about the environment. They had already chosen some places where they thought we might be able to get in touch with the right kind of people: the university, theatres, art galleries, the aquarium, the planetarium, etc. I was given the art gallery beat on the grounds that people with alternative ideas might turn up there. Anubhav was given the British Council Library; his face fell.

For the next four years, I became a familiar figure outside that art gallery, in blue jeans, green T-shirt and the cap with a dodo embroidered on it. I began to make friends with the other regulars: the chaiwalla, the pavement gallery artists from out of town. The square and the art gallery's big semi-circular building became my turf. Sunderabai, the woman who sold peanuts, became a friend who would give me a drink of water when I was thirsty and watch my bag when I went home for lunch. When I accosted some hapless soul coming out of the gallery with my forms, Sunderabai would move in to sell him some peanuts. At least one of us would score.

By the time I was in the twelfth standard, Sunderabai was sharing her lunch with me. Poor Anubhav didn't do as well at the British Council

Library. He had a bunch of stern policewomen to contend with and the hungry lawyers outside the nearby district courts. His enthusiasm soon waned.

That holiday, spent far away from the watchful eyes of relatives, gave me a taste for independence. I didn't feel the need to ask my parents for permission for everything I did. Aseem's humdrum world began to irritate me and I began to take off, to go trekking when I felt like it. What surprised me was that Tanay took my part. When I said I wanted to do zoo management, the parents were aghast. Science? For a girl? But Tanay was solidly on my side. Anubhav also took admission in science.

One day, as we were walking by the canal, on our way back from a film, Anubhav took my hand in his. I didn't pull away. Then he drew me close, put an arm over my shoulder. I felt a quiet thrill of excitement; something new was happening. Without speaking, we continued to walk along the canal. On the main road, however, he moved away immediately, putting some space between us.

The next time he was less timid. I went along because of that trickle of excitement. I let him kiss my cheek and a week later, my lips. I felt as if I were taking my first steps into a new world. Anubhav was no doubt enjoying himself.

I began to notice that he spent a lot of time in class just looking at me. The solicitude with which he bandaged my foot when I injured it on Sports Day drew a lot of attention. I began to wonder if he were in love with me or something.

One Sunday, I went to the hills to plant some fruit trees from seeds that Green Earth volunteers had collected. Anubhav was, naturally, with me. It began to rain in the morning and we were soon soaked. When we came back down, we ended up at Anubhav's bungalow. It was empty.

That was the first time I saw a male body nude. Anubhav's hands roamed my shoulders and breasts, gaining new ground at a victor's pace. In my turn, I tasted his entire body; and we satisfied our curiosity, exploring, investigating, fulfilling some old fantasies. I don't think I felt as much guilt as physical pain. And when that subsided, a feeling of victory, of achievement. Anubhav had got dressed immediately and gone off to sleep. I let myself out of the house. The rain-washed city seemed fresh and beautiful.

By evening, my heart had stopped thundering. When I telephoned him, he asked me over. I wanted to sit and chat with him in the old way but he drew me into his arms as soon as I walked in and said, 'I love you.'

I drew away and went to stand by the window. His eyes seemed to fill with tears but I felt it was the time to speak clearly and honestly.

'What happened between us was lovely. I enjoyed it but I only let it happen because I wanted the physical experience. I don't think I am in love with you. I think I might prove a difficult person to love. Let's just assume that bit is over.'

It was just as I feared. He walked out, banging doors as he went. I had to leave then and I walked home, trying to sort out what I felt. I had changed the rules. I had acquired a new vibe.

The only problem was that I couldn't share

these feelings. No one would hear me out in the right spirit. My female friends would have had heart attacks. It wasn't as if I was close to any of them. I had to hug my happiness to myself.

Anubhav's rage lasted a month. Then he said, 'I'll wait for you.'

'You're free to do as you please,' I replied. But I did want him back, as a friend.

When I met Anubhav, I understood why he was so uncomfortable. I was uncomfortable because of my ego. It had pleased my ego that he had been willing to wait. But I did not want him to see me in my condition.

Why aren't things easy? Or do we make them difficult?

31 July

As I went about the house when he was a paying guest, I would glance at the upstairs room. Tanay seemed to have become a full-time resident there. I'd see him from time to time, sitting in the window, his back to the world. He had always had his eye on that room. As long as he was happy, Aai-Baba didn't object. And since Aseem now had their room to himself, he was happy too. But still no one gave me permission to go upstairs.

Every Sunday, cupboards would be shifted around; nails would be knocked into walls. We could hear all this happen down under. I'd wonder: what was he doing upstairs? One Sunday, when Aai-Baba were out, I decided to find out. The room was locked; he was out too.

I stood there, taking it in, the colourful mats, the paintings on the walls. All this on his own? What could he not do to my room? What if he were to come and put things away, sort out my clothes, change the bedclothes, sweep, swab, organize the books? How much energy Aai would save if she didn't have to nag me.

At that point, he returned. He'd had breakfast at some Irani restaurant. He opened the door and invited me in.

'Nice room,' I said and went and sat down on the bed.

He ran his finger from his shoulder to his chest, looking meaningfully at me. I didn't get it at first until he smiled and did it again. Then I looked down at my shoulder; my bra strap was showing. The same bra. We both laughed until our stomachs hurt.

'I want to learn the guitar,' I said.

'Any time,' he said. 'You're always welcome.'

'Not here. That might get complicated.' He suggested the recreation hall at the art school; they even had a guitar there, he said. Good idea.

We chatted about this and that. He could cook and liked cooking. He knew French. He had guts. After his parents died, he had lived in hostels. He answered all my impertinent questions with a pleasant face. I asked him whether he painted in the way he did to mystify people. He didn't take it badly. He didn't defend his work, didn't explain it. From time to time, he did speak, but only a few relevant words. I had never met anyone like him. When I stopped blabbering and got up to go back downstairs, he said, 'You seem very curious about me?'

'Nothing like that, okay?' I replied and took the stairs, two at a time.

Then the board exams began and we didn't see each other. Examinations brought out the mother hen in Aai. Baba would stay up late to make me cups of tea or coffee. Aseem would clean the nibs of my pens and fill them with ink. Tanay would take me to the examination centre by bike and come fetch me. And I realized that these people, whom I saw as boring, were actually, fundamentally good at heart. They loved me and they tried to demonstrate it in this way.

That seems true even today. What if they hadn't taken me back when I returned? What would I have done?

I've only just understood what Sharayu Maushi used to say to me. That we were a transitional generation and that gave us several advantages. We had been given the freedom to choose how we want to live and behave. We were lucky to have parents who felt blessed in having children and were willing to take all the responsibilities that came with it. And so our sense of freedom is only a rehearsal. The next generation will have to pay the price.

1 August

I woke up way past noon. Aai and Maushi were in a huddle over some curtains that needed cleaning. I wandered about the house, and as I went upstairs, Maushi said, 'Anuja, what a lot of weight you've put on. Time to start exercising again.' Aai went off to get us some tea. It was a cloudy day; the terrace floor was cool. We drank our tea in companionable silence. Then it began to rain. Aai and Maushi hopped up, suddenly as animated as schoolgirls, and ran about, to rescue the curtains they had hung out to dry.

The phone rang. Anil Kaka's ship had docked in Sydney. Maushi and he chatted for a long time; she asked about his health, whether he was eating properly. Then she gave me the phone.

Anil Kaka suggested that I come and live with

them. He reminded me that they had once wanted to adopt me. He had gone on to the Negro spirituals CD he had bought me when the line was cut. I sat there, saying, 'Hello, hello' into the phone until Sharayu Maushi came and took it from my hand. Then she led me to the bathroom. I turned on the shower and sat on the pot, watching the steam rise.

I began to feel a touch of cabin fever. Perhaps I should go out? Pop in at the Green Earth office? I had a year on my hands before I went back to college. I ought to find some work. Whether he came back or not, I had to occupy myself. It was as if a light had been turned on inside my head.

The day after my twelfth standard board exams, I took up my place again, outside the art gallery, Green Earth forms in hand. I looked for Sunderabai, but the paanwalla said that she had gone back to her village, somewhere near Buldhana, because her daughter was about to deliver. In the middle of the pavement artists gallery, a young man sat on a stool, sketching people for a fee. I enjoyed my work but I also enjoyed watching the passing show. A bunch of Japanese students, a Parsi octogenarian, a famous newspaper columnist: all came out of the gallery.

I'd try to nab each one, give him or her a form, talk about Green Earth. As the columnist filled up the form, a press photographer took a picture of us.

By the afternoon, I was tired. I went to ask the paanwalla for some water. When I returned he was coming slowly down the stairs, one step at a time, as if in a trance. I went up to him.

'Excuse me sir, may I have a minute?'

'Cut to the chase. I don't have much time right now.'

So I gave him the spiel I'd give any other stranger.

'Do you know what just happened? They've given us dates for our student show. Oh yes, we have dates. After one year. And you're rabbitting on about the environment?'

I said, 'And what about the social responsibility of the artist?'

'Let us become artists first; then we'll see. But I can see my way to buying you a coffee,' he said.

'On one condition,' I replied. 'I pay for my own coffee. I cannot accept so much as a glass of water from someone who doesn't care about the environment.'

He laughed and shrugged.

I dropped my bag at a table in a corner and went to the counter to place my order. Behind the counter, I saw Shamim, an arts student. I must have looked surprised because he said, 'Summer job' as if in explanation. When I came back, he had picked up the guitar that the coffee shop had hanging on a wall and was playing. As always, I found myself staring at him. If someone stares into one's eyes for a long time, it makes one uncomfortable. So I tried to distract myself with the traffic, with the old lady, reading her book and drinking cold coffee. Halfway through playing the chords of 'Hotel California' he began to sing along. He had a nice throaty voice. Soon, he seemed lost in the song. And then my order was called out, my name attached. He stopped abruptly. Muttering, I went to get my order.

'You sing well,' I said when I got back to the table. 'Did you take lessons?'

'What a lot of questions you ask,' he said.

'I do, don't I?'

'Why?' he asked.

'I'm always curious about guys who can cook and play the guitar and have hairy chests and beautiful eyes,' I said.

I couldn't swear to it but I think he blushed.

The next day, I appeared in the newspapers with the columnist. I looked like a PT teacher. Overnight, I had become a star. Green Earth called to thank me. Other people called too. Anubhav came over with a cake. Aai marched into the kitchen and made shira.

'Have you all gone mad?' I asked. 'I just happened to be in the way.'

I went to take up my post outside the gallery. He came out of the gate of the arts school.

I could see the newspaper sticking out of his

bag. He came up and chatted about something else. He didn't mention the photograph.

'What are your plans for lunch? I thought I'd go to Baghdadi for a kheema pao,' he said. I left the forms with the paanwalla and went with him. I waited until we had eaten and were on the paan course. Wiping my reddened fingers on his shirt, I said, 'Saw the paper?'

'Which one?'

'The one in your bag.'

'Yes. Your photo's in the supplement. Have you seen it?'

I was startled, then angry. But he had already started talking about art school politics. That's when I realized he was different. And that I liked him.

The next morning, I was cleaning my toenails. Then I cleaned my ears. Tanay's cupboard had all sorts of interesting stuff ... ear buds, deodorants, cream with orange peel in it. I studied each one of the bottles and the pictures on them and then closed the door quickly. As I did so, I saw myself in the mirror. I took four steps back and looked again, carefully this time. There didn't seem to be much wrong but I thought: I must take care of myself. Tanay was out. So I opened his cupboard again. I took out some of the bottles and tubes but this was rocket science. I couldn't figure out what could be applied and where, how it was to be applied and to which part of the body, so I put everything back and shut the cupboard again. Never mind. I'm not that bad. I have what it takes in the proportions required. That will have to do.

I decided that I wasn't coming home for lunch; I'd eat with him. The only problem was that his school closed in a fortnight or so. He wouldn't turn up at the gallery then. It didn't work out quite like that. One day, he turned up at the gallery with four or five boys, all of whom also seemed to be bumbling about in a trance. His classmates, he said, and introduced me. Strange names they had: Vishwang, Orayan, Bahaar, Sahadev. Sahadev got to the point: 'We need a model to pose for us. Figure work. Would you?'

'Nude?' I asked.

'No, no,' Orayan said. 'We just like something in your face, something about your spirit.'

I thought about the face I had examined in the mirror earlier that day. Spirit, eh? Why not?

'What do I have to do?'

I'd just have to sit there. My shift at Green Earth ended at three o' clock. I agreed to sit for them between three and six.

'We can't pay you. Do you mind?'

I hadn't even thought there'd be money involved.

While this was going on, he was looking at one of the pictures of the pavement artists. 'In return, lunch will be on me,' he said. 'My company thrown in free.'

I began to laugh. I realized that I was over-reacting when even the doped out types began to look puzzled. I controlled myself and threw in a demand.

'And guitar lessons. You were going to teach me, remember?'

2 August

Today, I woke up early as usual. At seven o'clock, Sakhubai, who does the floors, was dragging a rusty table along the floor. The ugly sound brought on the goosebumps and total wakefulness.

I ran into the passage and shouted, 'Can't you lift that damned thing?'

Her face fell and I felt ashamed. I took one end of the table and helped her lift it.

Aai and Maushi came back from their morning walk. When Aai goes visiting, she wears only salwar kameez. Maushi's kameez flapped around Aai like a tent. She was wearing Maushi's canvas shoes too but still, the effect was rather pleasing. To top it all, she had a big fat kunku and a shiny mangalsutra on.

I got dressed and left and then was forced to return. I had no money. I hadn't needed any for a while. Aai took out some money and said, 'On your way back, can you get some shengdaana and sabudaana? It's Tuesday tomorrow and this Sharayu has nothing I can eat. Here's three hundred more. You don't have anything left, do you?'

It took me nearly an hour to get to the city. I walked around with no purpose, no intention, no direction. The shops were only just beginning to open. The chaiwalla was surrounded by college students. Traffic began to increase. Old men, sweaty from badminton, were chatting with their friends as they kick-started their recalcitrant bikes. My feet took me to the gallery. I thought I shouldn't linger, it might set me back. But then I felt: I'm tired of this fear. Let's see what happens.

I stopped at the chowk and looked around.

Within a few minutes, a young man arrived, wearing the familiar green T-shirt and cap of the Green Earth volunteers. He pulled out his forms and began to arrange them.

My stomach hollowed out. Only my life was on hold. Everyone else was going about their business. The honking of the cars started to worry me. I wanted to go home. He was gone. I turned quickly towards the terminal from where a bus could take me back to Sharayu Maushi's home. Every spot on the road began to remind me of him. The traffic roared past. The exhaust made me feel dizzy. I began to rush along, pushing past women shopping from the roadside vendors. I got into a bus that was as hot as a stove and returned home. I rushed to the bathroom and splashed my face with cold water, again and again, as if that would cool the heat inside my head.

When Aai came to call me for lunch, I was outside, watching the summer rain. I know now that I'm still not well. I should have listened to Aai. I asked her to cancel my afternoon appointment with Dr Khanvilkar.

In the middle of all this, Anubhav called. He had seen me that morning, walking past the tennis courts. He couldn't believe his eyes. Then he was upset that I hadn't gone to visit him. What could I say? He said, 'If you're coming into the city, just tell me. Why bump around in a bus?' This is the boy I taught how to ride a motorcycle. Has he forgotten that? Have I? I don't understand anything. This town seems like a big city sometimes and sometimes it's a village. You step out and bump into a dozen people you know.

I have started to feel that the friends you make in school, the ones you've known forever, begin to turn into fossils. They merge into their families, losing all identity. You don't know the new ones as much as you should. They can fool you.

Why can't Anubhav walk into my life as a new friend?

3 August

Orayan's father had a riverside bungalow. It was empty and it stood in for a studio through the vacations. It had glass windows six feet high. Evening light streamed slantwise through these windows. The walls were painted in different colours, courtesy Orayan. The floor was wood; it echoed under your feet if you had shoes on.

My twelfth standard holidays were spent in this room. Now, I didn't mind being banned from the upstairs room; after all, I was meeting him every day.

In the middle of the room, I sat on a variety of objects: on chairs, on stools, on paatis, on the floor and once on a ladder laid on its side. Around me, the trance team worked on their easels. He was right in front of me, all the time.

His eyes swung from me to the canvas and back, barely resting for seconds before shifting again. No one let me peek. Nor could I get up in between. After lunch, I would sometimes begin to drowse. I would fall asleep sometimes, quick catnaps, but since I didn't drop out of the pose, no one stopped working. I would wait for four to strike.

That was a break for tea, brewed on an electric stove. There was a coal stove outside. Sahadev would cook corn on the cob, spicing them and salting them and we would devour those too. Twenty minutes later, everyone would get back to work because they knew that on the dot, at six, I would be up and out of there.

At the end of the first week, they looked at each other's work. (They had decided this before starting.) I could not recognize myself in any of their paintings, except in Bahaar's. I told Bahaar, 'You're the only painter here. That looks like a photograph of me.' Wrong thing to say apparently. Bahaar's face fell and Sahadev started to smile but tried to cover it up. Then they started talking shop, the gobbledygook of art students.

The next day, I said, 'What's all this, sitting in a room and painting? Go out, enjoy nature, paint some trees and flowers and stuff.' The next Sunday, I was to take the children of the Zilla Parishad school on a river clean-up. At least, we'd clear up the banks of plastic. I told them, 'Take your boards and let's go. Draw me as I clear up the river.' And right enough, they all appeared on the banks of the river with their paraphernalia. They sketched for a bit and then began to help too.

By the time the vacation had ended, the trance bunch could have had an exhibition of portraits of me. I don't know what they learned or what they got out of it. They were practising.

I never saw those paintings again.

By the end of the holidays, I knew I was in love with him. It wasn't just a body thing. I'm not a halfway person. Either I love or I detest. Him, I loved. I loved his quietness, his understated way with words, his independence, his ability to respect your space. I had not fallen in love before so I couldn't even be sure that this was the real thing. As the vacations drew to a close, I began to think about this. Finally, I decided that there was nothing to be gained by putting a name to what I was feeling. Instead, I'd just get to know him better in my own way.

I asked him out to the movies a few times. But he said he didn't like the way Hollywood seemed hung up on a few themes: alien attacks, dinosaurs, violence, marriage. I didn't want to see Hindi or Marathi movies and that put paid to that.

One day, I popped him on the back of my bike and we blazed out of the city. We came off the ghats and hit the highway and coasted along. A mango tree, large and old, loomed up along the edge of the road. Next to it, a path led to some little village. It was about four in the afternoon. I parked the bike in the shade of the tree and we leaned against it. A little boy was playing in the mud. His mother was standing next to him, in brilliant colours, nail-enamel bright. Gradually, some more people arrived.

An old granny type in a nine-yard sari, two or three men who looked like Warkaris in their huge turbans, that kind. And then the State Transport bus arrived and they got in. Only he and I were left.

We hadn't said much to each other after we'd left the city. I hadn't climbed a tree in ages, so I clambered up until I was astride a branch. He grinned as I climbed swiftly. 'Come up,' I beckoned. 'No,' he shook his head.

I sat there, looking at the fields, the trees, the wells. After a while, he said, over a yawn: 'You want to say something? Why did you bring me here?' I had been waiting for this very question, I realized. If he asked me, I could tell him.

I told him everything. About myself, about Anubhav, about my feelings for him.

The sun was almost at the horizon by the time I finished. I sat on the tree and spoke and he sat by the road and listened. At first, I could see his expressions as I spoke but it grew dark and then I could only hear some vaguely encouraging grunts. I rambled on for nearly an hour or an hour and a half before I tired. That he could listen without speaking for such a length of time did not surprise me.

He only said, 'This is like something out of Jim Corbett. Evening and the hunter up a tree and the tiger waiting below. Only this tiger doesn't bite. Come on down.' I came down and started the bike. When he climbed on, he put both his arms around my waist and rested his chin on my shoulder. I said, 'Hello! I talked for hours and you're not going to say anything?' He began to sing, in French, I think. As we rode along the highway, now lit by headlights, he sang on. He sang into the breeze, he sang as we came into the city. He ignored the way people stared at him when we stopped for signals and he continued to sing. He ignored their mockery.

What had I gone and done? Had I proposed to him, as the girls in college would say, or what?

4 August

I refused to go back to the doctor. This talking isn't helping me at all. In the last month I've been for ten or more sessions. That should be enough. I don't want to be treated like a patient. I enjoy writing and for that, I have Dr Khanvilkar to thank.

Staying here annoyed me at the beginning; then it became a routine; now I've begun to like it. Maushi and Kaka had wanted to adopt me. If they had, this house with its artefacts from across the world, this room in which I am now, all this would have been mine, no?

This morning I asked Maushi, 'If I had been your daughter and I had done something like this, would you have sent me somewhere else for a change of scene?'

Aai was having her bath. Maushi looked at the bathroom door, took a deep breath and said, 'I would not have sent you away. Not even if it meant keeping you in a house where everything would remind you of a man. But the decision was your parents'; they asked me if I would have you and I agreed because I knew, at some level, you were also tired of your home. Otherwise why would you have left with that boy?'

I interrupted: 'Okay, the truth please. Does the doctor report back on what I tell her?'

'Not everything. Just what we need to know and what is related to the treatment. And it isn't as if we know nothing about you. You're not someone we met yesterday, you know.'

At this point, Aai came out of the door, a prayer on her lips, her wet hair wrapped in a towel. I left the room.

It would have been well-nigh impossible for me to tell my parents that I was in love with the paying guest. Perhaps they would have been able to listen without getting angry but they would have asked: why had I felt the need for secrecy? And then why had I left home?

That afternoon, Maushi and I looked at her wedding album. I couldn't recognize Aai and Baba. Aseem was in some of the photographs, asleep on Aai's shoulder. Tanay and I hadn't been born. Aaji and Ajoba were smiling in the photographs. It was as if they were sighing with relief. Anil Kaka sported a moustache and was wearing bell-bottoms and a shirt of a hectic floral pattern, Sharayu Maushi looked just the same. Perhaps it's because she never had kids, never had to raise them. That seems to keep a woman young. You could tell what had happened to Aai and Baba in the process of bringing us into the world and raising us.

That might be why I didn't tell my parents. They would have taken charge of everything and we would have lost control of our lives. They would have accelerated straight to the marriage hall. He would have been sat down and they would have demanded all kinds of confidences from him. They would have read me a sermon about the importance of education and how I should finish my degree before marriage. Then they would have hired a hall, called five hundred or six hundred relatives that no one had ever heard of and fed them and declared us married.

This is why I concealed even my friendship with him. Even when we went out together, I'd make him get off the bike at a traffic signal before the house. I did not visit him in the upstairs room. Anubhav saw all this happening; he knew. How could he not? His face was heavy and helpless with knowledge but I didn't have the words to explain. When these answers surfaced, I fell into a deep and lovely sleep.

The results came out. I got 89 per cent. I was delighted. I had planned on an MSc in the same college, after which I planned a master's degree in zoo management. I had no worries, no cares. When the holidays ended, I returned the Green Earth forms and my report. That year, they had decided to pay volunteers a stipend. Two thousand five hundred rupees! My first cheque!

I was over the moon. I thought I'd take everyone out to dinner.

'Can I ask him too?' I asked my parents. 'It won't look nice, leaving him out.'

'Okay,' said Aai. I bounced off to ask him. Once again, he surprised me. 'I'm not coming. We can go out on our own.'

After the family treat, I had four hundred rupees left. I said to Anubhav, 'I've decided that I want to taste beer and see. I've also decided that I can't do it alone. And I want to pay for it from my own earnings.' He was more than ready to come with me. On the way home from the beer bar, I felt light and happy. It seemed a wonder that I'd never drunk such a great thing before. I felt a great liquid love for the world surge through me.

That left two hundred rupees. Aai said, 'Give me that passbook. I'll put it in the locker with the others.' And so ended my spree.

But it was fun while it lasted, even the family dinner. At home, we didn't eat together, as a family. So it seemed odd for all of us to be at the table at the same time. Baba perused the menu with great care. Aai was telling me something about Prakash Kaka's Kanchan who was pregnant. Aseem was sending messages on his mobile. Tanay had bought me a Bon Jovi cassette. He gave it to me after dinner and left for parts unknown. And all of us went our separate ways, as if we weren't a family at all, just a bunch of friends saying bye to each other after dinner.

I had never been to a beer bar before. Okay, once with Orayan and Sahadev but I had had nothing to drink there. This time, I pressed the cold beer bottle to my face. The waiter stood there, opener in hand. When the bottle was opened, a whiff of vapour escaped. The waiter tilted our glasses and filled them slowly. I raised my glass and tried to clink it against Anubhav's but he said, 'You only raise your glass with beer.' Then he raised his and said, 'To your first salary.' I said, 'To my life, to my great life.' Then I closed my eyes and took a long deep swig. Five minutes later, the garlic mushrooms came. I nibbled and sipped and looked about.

The bar was packed. Cigarette smoke hung over us like fat clouds. Mario Miranda sketches on the walls. An old juke box in a corner. A great sense of fellow feeling for everyone in the bar swamped me. I stroked Anubhav's cheek. I got the feeling we were all sailing in the same boat. The boat was cutting through the waters, purposefully. But where were we headed? No one could ever know. Since we shared this common fate, it was incumbent upon us to love one another. Anubhav ordered another bottle and filled my glass. I pressed the glass against my lids and tried to see something in the darkness. Colours flashed and sparkled. When I opened my eyes, a man at the next table was pointing at me and laughing. I felt that I should invite everyone I knew to sit with me and drink ice-cold beer. No one should need to do anything else.

The treat I gave him? He said, 'I want bhakri and mutton rassa.' He knew where he wanted it too: Kolhapur Durbar behind the market yard.

'It costs nothing to eat there,' I said.

'Why does that matter?' he replied.

The place was full of peons and farmers and truck drivers. The tables were arranged as in a college mess. It took half an hour for us to be seated and we weren't even at the same table. But what food it was, what food. From his table, he demonstrated how to crush the bhakri into the rassa and eat it. We ate our fill, even as our breaths hissed wetly through our noses. Behind me some women stood, waiting for my seat. One of them patted my back and put a glass of water in front of me when it became apparent that my mouth was aflame with spices. Outside, pouring water over my hands from a tumbler, he said in the nasal tone of a thousand Brahmin aunties, 'So, Joshi? Still hankering for the sedate pleasures of rice and varan, ghee, salt-and-lime?' I laughed and wiped my hands on his shirt.

And then those golden holidays ended and the routine of college started again. Lectures, practicals right up to two o'clock and then freedom. In the beginning, I'd go to the art school and dig him out. But after a week, he got annoyed. 'I'm working seriously at my art. I can't be disturbed like this, every day. Go home. Go sow some seeds. But don't expect me to drop everything just because you're free.' I bridled. 'Sure. Keep at those abstruse canvases. Perhaps if you could paint something one could recognize, I might take your art a little more seriously.' He looked at me sardonically and laughed.

The next day he and Tanay went off somewhere and did not come back for two days. Aai said they'd gone to Tanay's friend's farm in Karnavadi. The cheek. Not a word to me. On top of that, no apologies and to add insult to injury, they took the bike too. I had to use the bus for two days. I felt I should go to that godforsaken village and drag him back by the collar. Half the day, he and Tanay were in each other's pockets. What need to wander off together?

When they returned, they brought home all kinds of farm produce. As if nothing had happened, he asked: 'Coming for a swim?' I didn't want to fight with him so I said, 'Sure.' And then it struck me that I was a goner. In those two days, I had thought of nothing else. I had let him and his ways get to me. It was the first time such a thing had happened. This just wasn't me.

7 August

I haven't been able to write for the last couple of days. Yesterday when I sat down at this desk, I thought I should read what I'd written up to now. Tanay has lots of books like this: the correspondence of So-and-So and Such-and-Such; the diaries of this person or that. When I read what I'd written, one thing became clear: this act of writing and reading what you have written helps you see yourself clearly. Writing this seems to have calmed me a little. As long as I can be sure it's private. Aai, if you're reading this on the sly, please don't. Put this book back where you found it and don't open it again.

It's been a month since I came home. Aai, I'm going to trust you. I'm assuming you've put this diary down. What a terrible month it has been.

It was as if my mind was fractured, the way a bone can be. My thoughts were a hairball inside my head. Now I'm beginning to be able to tease them out a bit.

I kept on reading and then I didn't feel like writing at all. I was taking a walk in the garden, when Baba puttputted up on the scooter. He had brought me some Rajgira laddoos. I crunched them until my teeth hurt.

'I am really feeling better now,' I told Baba. 'Now, let's put this behind us. I don't want to be treated as if I'm ill any more. I'm coming home.'

Maushi's face fell. So I quickly said, 'Or let's do it this way. You take Aai home now. Maushi will drop me off in a couple of days.' When they looked unsure, I added, 'I won't do anything to cause you a moment's worry.' Aai went off to get ready. She had been yearning to go back anyway. Her conversation was peppered with remarks like, 'Do you think he'll have eaten?' and 'Aseem likes a glass of warm milk when he gets back from work,' and 'The turmeric should have been ground today.' Aai had made both

these men—Baba and his carbon copy, Aseem—
dependent on her. For many years, I had noticed
that Aai would be working like a navvy all day in
the house: she would have shabby clothes on,
her forehead would be sweaty. But as soon as it
was time for Baba to return, she'd have a wash
and put on a nice sari. She'd get a hot snack
going for him. Just before he was to arrive, a
glass of sherbet would go into the fridge. The
house, already clean, would be given a once-
over. And when he knocked, she would open
the door with a smile. Everything was aimed at
that brief encounter at the door. Then the
drudgery of the day would return. Baba would
slump in front of the TV in his banian and
pyjamas. I often wondered why Aai would not
dress up for herself, just because she wanted to?
Or why didn't she just stay well-dressed all day?
But if this was her world, who was going to
disrupt it?

When she left with Baba, Maushi and I went
to the market. We bought crabs and ate them
until we could eat no more. All washed down
with sol kadi.

Yesterday, Maushi and I went for a walk. In her canvas shoes, short hair, T-shirt and tracks, she looked like she could be one of my friends from college. As she strode along, you wouldn't believe she was pushing fifty. She told me she was going to feel lonely once I left. Until Anil Kaka came back, she'd be alone. I asked why she didn't go with him.

'It's no pleasure cruise. It's like taking a holiday in your husband's office. He's always busy. And in the evening, the boys get together for a drink.' Maushi began to feel she was in the way, that he couldn't get on with his routine. So when they docked, she took a flight back.

On the way home, we stopped for tender coconuts. The coconut man seemed to know Maushi well. He chose carefully and the water was very sweet. A short distance away, there was a petrol drum for the husks. Two boys aimed their coconuts at the drum and missed. The coconut man said that he'd charge only half if anyone could throw their coconuts into the drum. 'Let's try,' I said. Maushi aimed and sent her coconut into the drum. I clapped. Then it was my turn.

'What's your secret?' I asked.

'Concentrate on something that will focus your mind,' she said.

I took aim and he appeared in front of the drum. I got it in and then jumped up and down and said, 'Instead of a discount, just give us another coconut.' Then we drank it together, like they do in the films, with two straws. When we got home, his face was clear in front of my eyes. I felt a deep sadness descend on me. There were no words.

This morning Maushi brought me home. I am sitting at my table in my room and writing this. We had a Marathi poem set for us in school. The poet suggested that the walls of your room know you best. As school children, we mocked the poem but now I wonder: what does my wall think of me? Does it wonder at this Anuja, who has returned after six months away and seems normal again?

After I came back, my parents took me to

Sharayu Maushi's house almost within two or three days. I didn't have time to look properly at the house. I haven't been away for more than six months but it seems like a new house entirely. The mess on the table, the clothes hanging on pegs, the things lying on the floor, all these have vanished. They've moved the television into my room. It's not my room any longer, it would seem. They didn't expect me back, it would seem, and they took over my space.

When Maushi's car came into the compound, I stepped out of the house and, by some chance, I looked up at the upstairs room. I blanked out. Someone was moving around there. Someone?

After lunch, Maushi went home; she gave me her Discman and a bag filled with about fifty of Anil Kaka's CDs. Then I thought to myself: I have to do this. After I had tea, I climbed to the terrace. At first, I thought Tanay must have taken the room for himself. But that wasn't it. It was a total mess. The cupboards hung open, their contents strewn on the floor. His paintings had been ripped and thrown here and there. His paint bottles had been scattered. Everything was covered with a layer of dust. In the middle of it all, an Irani restaurant chair, the kind with the round seat and four spindly legs, and on the rack, a big fat glass jar. Tanay must have assumed that I had been abducted or something of the sort and must have taken out his anger on these things. For a while, I couldn't stop thinking of him as I stood there.

I could see him as if in a series of images: working on a painting, cooking his food, listening to his Walkman, leaning out of the window to pluck chaafa flowers, playing the guitar. The intensity of my feelings seemed to have dulled a little. A list of questions began to form, questions to which no one could have any answers.

I sat down on the chair. If he had not wanted me to leave with him, he should have said so. Had I not given him enough time to think? Or did he assume that it was just a passing fancy for me? Perhaps that was it. He thought I was in for a good time and when he saw it was serious, he just had to get away.

Guesses. All guesses. He wasn't the kind of person who told you what he was thinking. Even our friendship had been based on my advances. If it had developed, it was because I had forced the pace. He had made no demands of his own. He had claimed no rights over me. He had never forced me to do anything I didn't want. Only on rare occasions did he get angry about my stubborn nature. But had I mattered to him?

Even after I left with him, we hadn't got together physically, even if our friendship had grown stronger. I had had enough experience not to feel any intense curiosity about these matters. I knew what it was. I had none of the usual feminine anxieties about it. Once, when I had come to the upstairs room, he had drawn me close to him and we had sat together for a long while. When I was sitting behind him on the bike, we were physically close, but most of the other time, it wasn't about that at all. With the exception of when he was teaching me the guitar. He would encircle me in his arms and we would play the chords together. I would breathe deep the smell of his body, rising as if off damp clothes. Once in a while, his stubble would scrape my face and arouse me. My hands would fumble the chords.

The only time he took the initiative was when we were by the sea. It had only been four days since we'd come to Pondicherry from Mudumalai. Now what? I had no idea. How were we to live? Where? I was the worrier; his face showed no concern. He had gone to the library so I left a note and took the cycle and went off to the beach. On that broad clean sweep of sand, I sat, looking out at a languid sea. I had no idea how long I sat there. Then he was there, sitting down beside me. The sun was dipping beneath the horizon and darkness was falling. He took my worried face in his hands and brushed his lips over my face.

I began to respond and suddenly the physical hunger we had ignored for days sprang to life between us. It was as I remembered, deeper, fuller because we cared about each other. My body was smeared with sand, sticky with mud, but that didn't stop him from caressing me, keeping me close in his arms. In the middle of the night, our bodies drifted apart. Later, the tide lapping against our feet woke us up. We got up, hunted up our clothes and, wheeling the bicycle, we returned to our room.

Outside, it was dark. In this haze of memory, I hadn't noticed the sun set. When I locked the room and came downstairs, Baba had returned from the office. So had Aseem. They were chatting and laughing together. As I went into my room, I saw Tanay sitting at the window, in the darkness.

'At least put on the light,' I said and switched on the tubelight. He turned to me.

'How are you? Good to have you back,' he said and then he came to me and began to weep. I said, in a panic, that I was never going to leave again. After a while, the tears dried up and he left.

When Aai came to call me for dinner, she said that Tanay had been hurt the most by my departure, that he had turned silent in grief. He had always seemed on the verge of tears. She had always thought that her children didn't really have strong bonds but she was pleased to see that he had been so deeply concerned.

As she went into the kitchen, she said, 'At the end of the day, it's family you can depend on. Blood is thicker than water.'

8 August

Baba kicking his scooter into life woke me at seven this morning. In the kitchen, Aai was banging the pots and pans as she washed up. Aseem was playing some Mohammed Rafi wail. I could hear him shout, 'Aai, bath water please,' and 'Aai, the tea's gone cold, warm it up,' and other such demands. When I came out of my room, Tanay was getting ready to go out.

'Off somewhere?' I asked.

'Somewhere? University! It's convocation day.'

So his results had been out for a while. Before I could ask how he had done, he had left.

Everyone left. Only Aai and I were at home. Aai was busy in the kitchen so I was actually alone. I realized I shouldn't be sitting around like this. Until I got admission next year I had to do something. My mind was in danger of rusting, if I just sat around.

In the afternoon, I went and joined a gym. I popped in at Green Earth on the way back. I waited for Sabina, a resource person, for an hour. Late in the afternoon, when she had not returned to the office, I left and came home. I called Neha. She had gone for a film with a friend. It was going to take patience to get back into the swing of things. Everyone had got on with their lives. I had thrown it all away to go off. I thought of calling Anubhav, picked up the receiver and then replaced it. That would be selfish of me. And so I sat there, until evening came, and I wondered: who wanted me back? Why had I returned?

At five, the phone rang. Aai said it was for me. It was Anubhav. He asked if I'd like to go for a walk in the university grounds. When we got off the bike, we walked in silence for a bit. Then we sat on a mound and he said, 'It's been a few days, right? If you need something . . . Even if it's just someone to talk to, just call, okay? I'm not about to ask any questions you don't want to answer.'

I just nodded. Why wasn't he like other men? Why wasn't he cursing me, screaming at me?

When he took me home again, I got off the bike and stood there, trying to find something to say. He fiddled with the keys of the bike and then turned it off and sat there. In the sudden silence, we looked at each other. Then he kickstarted the bike and rode off.

In the fifth or sixth standard, I forgot to take my lunch box to school. If anyone forgot, Anubhav would immediately tear his poli into two and share. So I ate his poli. I knew there was always a crunchy red apple in his bag and I seized that too and ate it. He never complained.

When Anubhav left, I entered the house to a familiar scene. Baba and Aseem were watching cricket. Aai was bumping about in the kitchen. Tanay was staring into space. I said nothing and went into my room and bolted the door.

In a minute, someone was knocking. It was Aai. 'Come and eat,' she said. Because Aai told me to eat, I ate. Because Baba told me to take my medicines, I took my medicines. Then I retreated to bed, covering myself with a sheet. The fan clinked and rattled as it stirred the air. The girls in Nadkarni's were playing antakshari. I couldn't sleep so I got up and sat down at my table and started to write.

When things got unbearable, I came home. If things had gone well, would they have ever seen me again? And why unbearable? Because I could not take care of myself? Because of my sick mind?

How had I imagined I would live without anyone by my side? I had planned nothing. Was that what went wrong? I should have sought independence. I should have thought to earn. I should have thought about saving. And then, I should have thought about a room of my own, however small. After a day's work, doing something I liked, I should be able to return to this place and relax in the manner of my choosing. Our house was big enough for middle-class dreams but not for privacy. I wouldn't even clean this room that I would have, if I didn't feel like it. And I'd have lots of greenery.

I had even told him about these plans. He had said, 'You are complete in yourself. You're so clear about what you want.' I had felt a rush of pleasure at his praise. I had not thought to ask him what his plans were.

I had another dream, which I'd fulfilled in Pondicherry. I had begun reading English books and, finally, I had even begun to decipher the American accent. I was in awe of how kids in those books and films would think up ways to earn some money doing small jobs for other people during their holidays. I had always dreamed of being a waitress.

So when I met Madame Eveline in the bazaar at Pondicherry, she appeared to me like a wish-fulfilling goddess. She was standing in front of a fisherwoman, carrying her wooden basket, slippers on her feet but a slash of red lipstick too. She brought each fish close to her face as if she were examining it for clues. The fisherwoman did not seem bothered; this seemed to be a daily

performance for her. Then she saw me and
began to chatter away in Tamil. I stopped her
and asked in sign language how much the fish I
wanted was going to cost me.

Madame Eveline stepped in and began to give
me advice in English. She dropped everything
and began to choose fish for me. I began to
protest but the fisherwoman caught my hand
and signalled me to let Eveline do what she
wanted. The old woman began to sort through
the prawns until she had chosen the best for me.
The fisherwoman's board was messy, as was the
sickle with which she sliced fish. Next to her, a
cat was eating the offal. I thought the old lady
was a little mental but she wasn't. She was just a
loving, eccentric and determined old lady. But
this I only discovered later.

I had no money with me then. What I had
brought with me was over. I had to ask him for
money for every little purchase I had to make.
He never gave me his wallet—not even to make
things easy for both of us. Nor did he ever go to
the market; but when I asked for money, he'd
give it to me.

After she had selected the fish, Madame Eveline asked me in her French English, 'Do you make the cooking?'

'No, I can't. My partner can, though. He's quite good.'

'My partner makes fish well too,' she replied. 'And he keeps my little fish happy too.'

She winked and laughed loudly. I could only stare at her.

We walked together to the road. Her 'partner' was waiting for her in a jeep. He looked about seventy-five years old. His name was Philip, he said. They had opened a restaurant in the ground floor of their home. They ran it together; he cooked and she sat at the counter, was the chief waitress and also cleaned the place. They had about twenty tables, they said. Only one or two dishes were on the menu, based on what Madame Eveline found in the market. The menu was then written in chalk on a blackboard. She enjoyed doing that, she said. But, 'Philip often forgets what has been written on the board and cooks something else. And then we fight.' So

now she had another board hanging in the
kitchen. They needed some help. They had had
two young women living on the premises but
had been forced to dismiss them.

'Why?'

'They were stealing,' said Madame Eveline.
'Grain. Money.'

I got into the jeep and said, 'Show me your
restaurant.'

When I returned to our room, I told him that
I had decided to take a job. No, that I had taken
a job. 'Great,' he said. 'Now you'll have
something to do.'

And I did indeed have something to do for
the next four months, morning and evening. I
suffered through that dream of mine.

Tomorrow, I must go to Green Earth and
meet Sabina. I have to do something for myself,
of myself; and I have to live the way I want to
live. Whatever it takes. And when it comes to
that, what else had I been doing in the last few
months?

The last few months have been odd in the extreme but they have sped by. I haven't been writing. I haven't felt like it.

I've been exercising every morning. Warming up for the gym with a jog, I realized that my stamina is shot. Three rounds and I was pooped. I couldn't manage much that first day. But when I returned to the bike, wiping the sweat from my face with a napkin, I felt fresh and revitalized, as if I had given my mind a workout too. I got home and went to work, reorganizing my room. I dragged the television out into the hall. Took the bags of grain out and dumped them in the kitchen. Ignored Aai's comments and complaints.

In the afternoon, I went to Green Earth again. Sabina was really happy to see me. 'Where have you been? We need some passionate people around this place.'

I said, 'Sabina, I need a job. A full-time job. I

don't mind if it's a lot of hard work. Or more responsibility. I have to support myself now.'

'Relax,' she said. 'I was about to suggest that. It's a field-work job, full-time. We throw in the training. Interested?'

I wanted to weep. (This keeps happening. Sorry.) Someone needed me, my eyes, my intelligence, my hands and legs. I wiped my eyes on my T-shirt and said that I was.

The family protested. No, that's not accurate. Aseem abstained from comment. My parents declared their opposition. First, I should finish my MSc, my health was not what it should be, that kind of thing. Baba kept up a steady rattle of protest. I tried to explain it to him.

'I feel fine now. I think I'll feel awful if I keep sitting around doing nothing.'

'Do what you want after we get you married. Then you don't even have to stay here. Fight with your husband over whether you should work or not. But if you're going to live here, you have to follow the rules,' he said.

So they had only been waiting for me to get well so that they could marry me off? I lost it.

'Where do these hoary old ideas come from?' I shouted. 'Marriage? My marriage? What gives you the right? What did you do with your life? Got married, had children, then what?'

He was so incensed he started forward to slap me. Aai got in the way. She calmed him down and sent him into another room. Then she came and slapped me and then went with him. Tanay was watching all this, his face the usual picture of sadness. 'I'm back, for heaven's sake,' I said. 'You can call a halt to the mourning now.' He said nothing and went into his room. I went into mine and bolted the door.

In the morning, gym. Afterwards, I ate what I was served in silence. I read the newspaper and at 11 a.m. I was at the office, with Sabina. As the day proceeded, as I looked at slides and listened to briefings, made notes and asked questions, the family and its discontents began to fade. I had two weeks of training and then an interview. If I cleared that, the job was mine. I threw myself into the work and when I left in the evening I was dog-tired. As I was leaving,

Sabina thrust three folders into my hands. 'Statistics on the pollution levels at the city chowks, the debates that have been held in the Municipal Corporation and their decisions, and this one on dumping into the river. Bedtime reading,' she said.

That morning I'd called Sharayu Maushi and said I'd come over for a chat; but I had no energy left. I walked home through the crowds and the dust. As I crossed one of the bridges, I looked down and saw that it had shrunk to a trickle. The water was dirty and there was rubbish floating in it. I had the data in the files in my hands. That night, I lay in bed with the papers spread out in front of me. It was good sound work, data collected with much trouble and much commitment. There were newspaper cuttings. It was the city's health report, an X-ray of its interior.

After a few days, it began to dawn on me that this NGO work was rather pleasant and somewhat superficial. We had a posh office, we had air tickets at our disposal and very little real work. But they did seem to take trouble as well to fight for the causes they cared about. Two of my colleagues had master's in social work. One of them was an idealist, sincere if aggressive in manner. The other was focused on his career. He was the kind who had turned up here perhaps because he hadn't got admission into the MBA programme he wanted. Our seniors were a varied bunch of people. All along, I'd been a volunteer so I'd never worked inside the office and I didn't know any of them. But the training was fun.

One day, I didn't have anything more to do by three thirty or four. A young man called Ashwamegh had come from Delhi to make a presentation. He had a flight to catch and had to leave. I was like a child let out of school; I rushed off to Sharayu Maushi's house.

She listened carefully, attentively. I called home to tell Aai I would have dinner with Sharayu Maushi and she said, 'Sure. Eat there. Why don't you live there? After all, you don't want to live with us, at least not the way we'd like you to live.

Stay with her. She behaves like someone your age. A good pair you'll make.'

Maushi and I took chairs on to the terrace. 'You've changed,' she said. I looked at her questioningly. 'No, you've recovered. I can tell from your face.' I brought her up to date with my life after I had left her home and, when I had finished, she went downstairs and came up with a bottle of red wine, two glasses and a bunch of keys.

'You're well now,' she said. 'Time to celebrate.'

She poured us both glasses and handed me mine. Then she gave me the bunch of keys. I looked at her.

'First take a sip. Then we'll talk about the keys.'

In my eagerness, I took a great big gulp of wine. Not Sharayu Maushi. First she swirled the wine about and stared into its red dark heart. Then she brought it to her lips and took a sip so infinitesimal it could not have even wet her lips. Then she closed her eyes and I could sense the wine percolate through her.

'Our flat in the city is vacant. You can live there, if you want. Keep the keys. Then you can make your decision whenever you want.'

That was ten days ago. The keys are still in my bag. They come to hand every time I look for something.

I got home late that night. It must have been about twelve thirty or one. When Baba opened the door, he began to shout, as is now his wont. I didn't let what he was saying affect me at all. I waited him out. Now, when Aai or Baba shouts, I simply turn off their sound. It's as good as a 'mute' button.

Sunday. Aai and Baba got all dressed up. Tanay made tea for me. When Aseem came out in a formal shirt, doing up the buttons on his sleeves, I asked, 'What's up? Where you off to so early?'

He grinned and went off to put on his shoes. Aai had her pearl bangles on and held out her arms. Baba fixed the tiny screws that held them together.

'Where are you lot going?' I asked.

'Do you pay no attention to what I say? I told you about it yesterday. A proposal has come from the Chitpavan Sangha. She's a Sane. Aseem liked her photograph. When I told you about it, you were sitting there like a dummy. Aseem was bothered about having an unmarried younger sister in the house so I was asking you what you had decided to do. We thought you should get married and step out of his way. But would you answer? Would you say anything? So I said why should we let her interfere? Let's go and see the girl tomorrow. Let's finalize things if he likes her.'

Baba did not even smile when he looked at me. The three of them went off. Tanay and I were left, sitting at the table. His face wasn't sad as it usually was now, just blank. He hadn't shaved. He was glancing through the newspaper, one foot up on a chair.

'Good tea,' I said.

'Hmm.' He didn't raise his head from the paper.

'What's happening in your life? You haven't talked to me properly in days.'

'I have a friend in Mumbai. He's going to translate one of Manto's stories and turn it into a play. I'm going to assist him on it.'

'You're going to live in Mumbai?'

'From next month. Amrish says I can live with him in his flat. There's no one else. And I'm going to assist an ad film-maker on a new campaign. It sounds like something I might want to do. Let's see.'

Then he dropped the newspaper and went out.

It seemed as if all three of us were on a railway station with our bags, heading in different directions. If Tanay had been pining for my return, why was he behaving so badly now?

In the afternoon, I opened the doors to Maushi's flat. I had come here once before, for the Vastu Shanti pooja. Who knows why they had bought such a large flat? There was a layer of dust everywhere. It had almost everything one could need in terms of furniture, as far as I could make out since all of it was swathed in dust covers. The air was foul. When I went into the bedroom, I discovered why. One of the windows had a broken pane. And a sparrow had got in and built a nest on the ceiling fan. I backed out and walked through the flat, opening all the doors. Then I threw open the French windows and walked on to the balcony.

The green of the hills was in front of me and beneath me, the housing society's swimming pool. I sat on the balcony and stared out, the keys in my hand, confusion in my head. I wasn't sure I could do what I wanted to do.

Today when I sat down to write and put the date on the page, I began to wonder: why do I insist on this date business? Why must I put time stamps on everything? I thought of his dateless diary, the book in which he trapped memory. It was a beautiful book; I think he had covered it himself with some cobalt blue khadi cloth he had bought. He would write in it, sitting on the floor, his knees drawn up to his body, as a child might do his homework. Once I sneaked up behind him to see what he was writing. It was a 'to do' list.

'But how will you know when to do them?' I asked. 'You need a diary with dates.'

'When I want to do something, I'll do it. Why do I need dates?'

I did not ask him why he needed a list then.

When I was young, I did not have a doll's house or any long-legged foreign dolls. I knew vaguely that my friends had dolls and that they dressed them up and played house for hours on end without getting bored. And when they had finished, they would talk about their dolls. I was a bit of a tearaway, or so Aai maintains. Nadkarni Kaku's nephews would visit when they had holidays. One of them was Manoj. I once made a nice and drippy ball of dark brown mud and gave it to Manoj, saying it was chocolate ice cream. He even ate some. That night his stomach swelled up and there was much commotion next door as he was taken to a hospital.

I enjoyed making forts. Aseem and I would take spades and buckets and get ourselves some good squidgy mud from an empty plot down the road. Aseem would dig it all up and I would make several trips, back and forth, with the mud. Then we would raise our walls and decorate them with stones and suchlike. By night, my fort would be ready. I would plant some seeds as crops so that by the time Diwali came, the fields inside the fort would be coming along nicely. Then on Bhau-Beej, the day after Diwali, we would blow up the fort with sutli-bombs.

When I got to the eighth standard, Aai began

to ask me to do kitchen stuff: cut those onions, fry those papads, start the veggies off. She'd wake me up and ask me to make tea. By the time I was in college, I was doing odd bits of work for her. But I found the work very boring.

The food I cooked showed my disinterest. When she tried to force me to learn cooking, I fought with her for the first time. I didn't win; how could I? I did learn some cooking but I also decided that, when I grew up, I wasn't going to be the one doing the cooking.

When those keys nudge my hand inside my purse, these things come back.

He cooked very well. He had had a hotplate when he lived upstairs. He cooked up various dishes on it, dishes from various countries, dishes whose names I had never heard of before. When we reached Pondicherry, it was about 7 p.m. I stayed with the luggage while he went to look for a place to stay. He returned in an hour, tired, and picked up his bag and began to walk. He beckoned me to follow. The room was in the basement of a building that saw a constant stream of tourists, both Indian and international. It was just right for us. It had a kitchen and some basic utensils.

He put down the luggage and went out again. He brought back some veggies and some rice and other necessities. While I was having a bath, he got some delicious pitla-bhaath ready. Memories of home came back and I hugged him as he stood there, dishing up. He made the next morning's tea and lunch too. I swept and swabbed and went out and got us a couple of cycles on hire. Those were my contributions to our housekeeping.

That evening, he went out and came back after having had dinner somewhere. I had been waiting for him.

'What's this?' he asked. 'You're here? I thought you'd have gone out somewhere too.'

I didn't understand this but I didn't say anything. I drank water and tried to go to sleep. But of course, I couldn't sleep and I got up and looked out at the houses in the street.

In the next few days, he got himself some

paints, brushes and an easel. They materialized, it seemed, one morning. I opened the door and there they all were, scattered about the room. I thought he'd put them away himself and left them alone. But when he came back, he picked up a book of poetry and lay about, reading it. Then we played the guitar together for some time and fell asleep. For the next two days, his art materials lay around. When they got in my way, I tried to impose some order.

I wanted to call Anubhav to bring him up to date on everything I'd been doing: the job applications, the training. I didn't even know his telephone number had changed. When I got the right one, the domestic help picked up the phone and shouted, 'Woo is spikking?' When I told her, I heard several voices begin a discussion.

She had obviously taken the cordless phone to Anubhav's door. On the way, I could hear the news on television, the call of street vendors, Kaku saying, 'At least take his tea and go . . .' When I heard loud music, I knew that the phone was at his door. 'It's Anuja,' I heard someone say. 'Do you want to talk to her or should I say you're bathing?' He grabbed the phone and shouted, 'Hello,' with a wealth of joy in his voice. He was delighted that I had taken the initiative and called him after so many months.

Today was the last day of training. Sabina was so enthusiastic that I felt the job was mine for the asking.

'Now it's just the interview,' Sabina said to me. 'And I think you should get past that easily. It will count that you've volunteered for so many years with us. Just speak confidently and clearly. I think it should be a breeze but there's one German lady on the panel. She might be a bit of a problem.'

'Don't worry, Sabina,' I said. 'I'll give it my best shot.'

On my way home, I began to wonder about this job. It wasn't what I had planned. I had wanted to study zoo management and become India's Gerald Durrell. This wasn't quite the same thing but at least it was related.

When I told him about my zoo dreams, we

were sitting on the beach. He listened to me and said, 'Sounds like a suitable job for you. You like pigeonholing people, classifying them and governing them accordingly. You'll do exactly that with your animals.'

I thought he was joking but, when I looked up at him, his face was serious. Then he got up, took off his clothes and went for a swim.

Most of the good memories I have of him are from the time before I left home with him. What happened to our time together?

I knew what I wanted. I wanted to live with him. I wanted him all to myself. I had my priorities clear. What were his priorities?

When we got to Pondicherry and started living in the same room, it occurred to me that I now had my wish. He would be with me, twenty-four hours of the day. But slowly, it also occurred to me that there were many dimensions to his personality that I did not know about.

For instance, he would listen quietly but then he would do as he pleased. Once he'd started on a painting, he could be silent for days. In the middle of the night, if the mood took him, he would go jogging. I tried to take all this in my stride; I had some weird habits too. I began to work in Madame Eveline's restaurant and started to earn some money. No longer did I have to ask him for money each time I went out. Why didn't that count? When I got back from work, I would tell him everything that had happened in the restaurant. He would have a hot meal ready for me and would tell me about his day. Every Saturday night, despite my protestations, he would rub warm oil into my hair and, on Sunday morning, wash it out again. He never said a word about the stains I left on his T-shirt.

Then Mme Eveline decided I was a thief too. I left in a huff. He was at home, cleaning up. When I told him what had happened, he didn't even lift his head from the task at hand.

'Okay,' he said.

Perhaps I had never understood him. If I think about it, those six months didn't amount to a very long time together but we seem to have made the most of it.

I had come a long way from home but I was not sure if I had done the right thing. In the first few days, I couldn't tell for certain. In the remaining days, it often felt like the right thing and as often it felt like a huge mistake. I would sit on the kitchen counter as he cooked or stand with him by the sea and tell him stories about my childhood. If homesickness washed over me, I'd put my head in his lap and stay there. As for him, he might well have been born the day he arrived to stay with us, for he never talked about his past.

His best gift: the guitar lessons. We'd draw close to each other anywhere—at home, on a hill, by the road, sitting on the beach, in a bus— and play the one and only guitar we had between us. Often we were singing in different pitches or we were out of tune, but we were together.

Now if I am to make my own accounts, I think I came out ahead if I discount my inability to understand him. He must have suddenly found that what he was doing, how he was living, no longer suited him. That was when he left. What

I am doing now, he must have done then: taken stock and made a decision.

Once you start living together and you see the same person day in and day out, you begin to wonder: was it for this I struggled and toiled? Did he feel that way? If he didn't, then why did he put his mattress on the floor?

I see myself as an independent thinker, a free spirit. When I was leaving with him, it did not occur to me to tell my friends anything. Whether I was aware of it or not, whether it happened because of something I did or not, I must have represented a restriction on his freedom.

Why do we judge relationships only by their age? Why is it that only a long-lasting relationship may be called successful? Now I no longer feel like weeping over him. I just want to meet him once, to ask him why. Then I look at Anubhav and I think: what explanation? From whom? What will I gain by holding him responsible? So maybe it's all for the best if he doesn't show up.

Aseem's wedding has been fixed. I had gone to a bookshop with Anubhav and, when I got home, I knew something was up. Aai had a big smile on her face when she opened the door. Baba was talking animatedly to Aseem on the phone. Why was he so well-dressed at home? Because the girl's father had just left.

Her name is Supriya. Aseem liked her but their horoscopes had to be matched. Their astrologer had just delivered himself of the good news that there was nothing in their stars to prevent the marriage and so her father had come to see us. Baba had no room in his head now for me; he was so thrilled that he fed me pedas with his own hands. Tanay picked up the receiver and congratulated Aseem. Aai fed Tanay with some pedas and blessed him. 'Now I have one daughter-in-law. If I get another one as nice, this house will fill up.' I looked around at the furniture and wondered whether it wasn't filled up enough. I picked up the receiver, obviously we all had to talk to Aseem, and said, 'Come home quick.'

Supriya is some months younger than me. She works in the accounts department of a pharmaceutical company. She earns eight thousand rupees a month. As Aai told me all this, I flashed back to one of Sabina's folders. This was one of the companies polluting the river. Green Earth had filed a case against them. Supriya likes cooking and meeting her relatives. Every Sunday she goes to learn how to make colourful candles. She is the only child. Her father has a bungalow. He is a retired police officer. She will bring twenty-five tolas of gold. She's a bit thin but that will be dealt with after marriage. The marriage has to happen quickly. Next week, engagement; next month, wedding. I said, 'Think about the cost.'

But the girl's father had said, 'It's the first important function in our family. We will do it all ourselves.' Since the marriage is to be conducted on Vedic principles, it will not take much doing. Four hundred relatives from our side and five hundred from theirs, think nothing of it. There will be a dandiya night before the wedding but no reception.

Everyone was opposed to the idea but I said

we should say on the wedding card: no gifts. We ought to move with the times. When Aai was telling Nadkarni Kaku this, Aseem returned from the office. And ooh, what a coy little boy he became! And Aai turned into a bundle of maternal love, blessing him and banishing the evil eye; and then, to top it all, Baba took out his expensive fountain pen and tucked it into his pocket! It was a nice little circus.

Tanay? As he was, he remained: blank and uncaring. That night, Aai asked us all to have dinner together and made the polis herself. Because Aseem liked shira with raisins, she made that too. Baba said to Aseem, 'Let everything go off well. If you need anything, just say the word. And just because you have a flat, there's no need to shift there immediately. Tell your Supriya to bear with her in-laws for a bit.'

'You have a flat of your own?' I asked Aseem.

'Not yet. But I've been thinking about it. Now that everything's fixed, I think I should. The loan will also be approved quickly.'

'If you want to know what happens at home,

you have to stay at home, Anuja,' Aai shouted from the kitchen where she was rolling a fresh batch of polis. I let it drop.

Supriya came home. Her mother and father came and a boy, around twelve years old. We didn't know who he was. 'This is our Mukul,' said her mother and that was all. Supriya was pretty in a coastal Maharashtrian kind of way. She was wearing a printed salwar kameez and only touches of make-up.

'You travel a lot, don't you?' she said to me. 'Trekking and all? Aseem was telling me.'

She spoke exactly like our handicrafts teacher in school: with gaps between sentences, even between phrases. She would say 'Fold your glazed paper,' but even that utterance would be divided into two. She was a well-read person and intelligent but she simply spoke that way. I thought the coloured candles looked boring. When Tanay shook her hand she blushed. She made the tea. She served everyone and then came into my room to serve me. Aseem returned at five thirty and they went out together. Four

proud parents and one bored Mukul went off
to look at halls and book one.

The atmosphere in the house changed radically.
Aai had something new to bother about. She
could no longer be bothered with my job, the
interview, where I was going and when I was
returning although she kept up a perfunctory
level of interest. Sharayu Maushi came regularly
to the house to help her with the wedding
arrangements.

Only then did I feel like staying at home. The
smell of new clothes is beautiful. Yesterday,
Sharayu Maushi dragged me off to go shopping.
I couldn't tell whether we were in the lobby of a
hotel or in a sari shop. I wasn't as bored as I
thought I would be. Aai had brought a list with
her but Sharayu Maushi chose some saris for
me at the speed of light. Then we went to the
jewellery shop. I wandered about looking at
things. Aai called out to me, 'Do you want
something?'

'No,' I said.

Aai began to talk again, until Sharayu Maushi

stopped her. She began to sort through the bangles and necklaces and put aside what we wanted. Her hands were swift and sure. We had the whole wedding shopping business done in two hours flat.

'I have to go to the temple. You go on ahead,' said Aai.

Maushi and I took a rickshaw, but she didn't direct him homewards. Instead, we went down a road past the Gymkhana to a leather goods shop in an old bungalow.

'I'm going to get you something for the wedding.'

There was a really lovely bag with a price that made me dizzy. That was what Green Earth was going to pay me as a starting salary. But I could see myself going to the interview, the bag over my shoulder. I'm wearing jeans and a jacket, sunglasses on my head. When I got home, I took the bag straight into my room because I didn't want any discussions about it.

The saris were all over the house, as they had to have their pallus done and falls put on them.

That wonderful dry smell filled the house. I picked one up and inhaled deeply. Aai misunderstood immediately. 'I said, didn't I? I said, get yourself a sari. Did you listen? No, you didn't. Don't you dare turn up for the wedding dressed like a tramp. The least you can do is wear a Punjabi suit.' But then Nadkarni Kaku arrived and she was given her invitation and thankfully Aai stopped talking about me.

I got onto the bike, and Anubhav and I whipped through the city. When we were near home, I said, 'I don't feel like going home.'

'Come and have lunch at mine,' he said.

His parents were at home. I began to feel a little ill at ease. So I left and had noodles from a cart and went to sit by the river. There was a bitter smell coming off the water. I thought Anubhav would follow but he didn't. I think he had really wanted me to eat at his place; he kept insisting but I couldn't stay. I wandered around the city for half an hour but when the petrol began to run out I went home.

Aai opened the door. I shut off my hearing

but she said nothing. She had a pen and a list in her hand. Baba was sitting on the sofa in his torn banian, punching figures into a calculator.

I went into my room and lay down. Tears began to fall but silently, so silently that when Aai came into the room to cover me she did so without even seeing that I was crying.

On the actual day of the interview I felt no apprehension. I filled up the new bag with my stuff: a pen, my resumé, the files that I had accumulated during training, a calculator, a small bottle of water and some paper. I left without telling anyone anything.

I pushed past the glass doors, climbed the stairs. Sabina saw me and came to wish me well. When I got there, the first young man was going in. I sat down on the sofa and began to play with the bag's zip.

The interview seemed easy; it lasted half an hour. I went to a coffee shop afterwards. Had I said what I wanted to? What interpretation would they put on my somewhat awkward sentences?

At home, Tanay's bags were packed. Baba was nowhere to be seen but Aai looked unhappy. Tanay appeared with a book in his hand. He stuffed it into the bag and, putting on his slippers, went to the upstairs room.

Baba came out of the inside room. He put some sachets of sacred ash into Tanay's bag. From Aai's lamentations, I discerned that Tanay was on his way to Mumbai. He didn't seem to have told them anything about his friend, the Manto play or the ad film-maker. In the morning, he had received a phone call and then he had told them that he was going to Mumbai and he had begun to pack. Aai couldn't believe it; with the engagement in two days! He had assured her he would return for it; he'd come in the evening and return in the night. Aai was full of questions and doubts: how would he live? What would he eat? He didn't know much about the city, hadn't visited it much. Would he manage in those crowded local trains? Baba seemed unfazed. Perhaps I had made him immune to this sort of behaviour from his children.

Tanay came down the stairs and entered the house. I thought he had forgotten something upstairs but he had nothing in his hands. His face was, as usual, blank but, now that I was looking at him, I could see dark rings under his eyes. I hadn't looked at him for so long, hadn't really looked. I felt bad about it. I tried to reach out, put my hand on his shoulder: 'You have the address, no? As soon as you've reached, call.'

He nodded.

'When will you be back?'

He said nothing.

Aai gave him a bottle of water. His haversack over his shoulder, another bag in his hands, he went to the door.

'I'll wait for your call,' Aai said, not moving.

Baba took the bag from him and went with him to the rickshaw. I watched them as they walked away: Baba moving slowly; Tanay clipping along, his head cocked. Then they turned a corner and vanished from my sight.

'At least he could have waited for the engagement to get over,' Aai said through sobs. 'Where will he stay? What kind of plays will he do?' I went and looked at the notepad that was kept by the phone. On it, there was an address:

Amrish Dubash, 5, Summer Queen, Arthur Bunder Road, Colaba. Aai read it over my shoulder.

'Dubash?' she asked.

'Parsi,' I said.

'Now when did he start having Parsi friends? That's all you lot are good for: to dump some more tensions on my poor head.'

At seven that evening, Tanay called from Mumbai. I answered the phone. He had arrived safely. He was at the address he had scribbled on the notepad. He said, 'Because it's you, I'm saying this. I won't be coming for any engagement shit. Rehearsals start tomorrow. And I have to find a job.'

As he was speaking, it seemed like he had received a jolt and he began to talk to someone in English. I told him about the interview at Green Earth. He wished me and hung up. As I was going into my room, Aseem said, 'When Supriya and her folks are around, could you please wear salwar kameez? For my sake. Until the wedding is over.'

The engagement happened. I have no idea what happened exactly. Aai and Baba kept waiting for Tanay. The house was flooded with relatives. Everyone came up to me, to stroke my face solicitously, in the hope of extracting some juicy details. All of them approved of Supriya, except for Durga Aji. She said, 'Whatever you say, Aseem is a little better than she is.' That night, Ram Kaka, Prakash Kaka, Baba, Supriya's father and her uncle sat down to a bottle of whisky. Supriya's uncle got drunk and began to act up. The girls from the Nadkarni Hostel came into the balcony to watch. He was brought into my room and put to sleep on my bed.

The day before the engagement, two workers were talking to Baba in the courtyard. All three went upstairs. Durga Aji had ordered the upstairs room cleared for the influx of guests. I watched from the window. 'Don't stand there. Go somewhere else,' I ordered my feet but they remained stubbornly rooted to the spot.

Rolls of canvas, an easel, the two paintings on the wall, a tattered lampshade, a mat, a bucket, a bundle of clothes, a hotplate, a broken strainer, two glass plates, spoons . . . thick with dust, they were brought down by the workers. The glass jar broke on the way down; shards flew everywhere. Carrying an Irani restaurant-style chair, one of the workers came to the door. 'This is in good shape. Do you want to keep it?' he asked. Before I could say anything, Aai said, 'Throw it all in the rubbish. Burn the rest. I don't want even a thread from that room in my house.' And so they swept the room clean. Then they hosed it down, and a stream of blue water erupted from the door of the upstairs room and flowed down the stairs.

The day after the engagement, the phone rang. Sabina's voice came ringing down the line. I had got the job. I felt like I was floating. The other women were asleep in the room upstairs. I called to Sharayu Maushi. She came out with a cup of tea in her hand. I called her down and told her my news. She was delighted.

I got my appointment letter and sat the parents down. Baba said, 'What about your MSc?' I replied, 'Next year. This is work I like and I'm going to do it. And since we're sitting here and talking like this, I should tell you that I have decided to live apart. In Sharayu Maushi's flat. I think I'll feel better there. It's not that there's anything wrong with staying here, with you. But I think this is what I should do.' I knew what their arguments were going to be already so I tuned them out.

I haven't brought much stuff with me. My clothes, of course. My certificates, photographs, music. I left the bike behind. Since Aai was angry, I didn't think she'd help me. Sharayu Maushi brought in enough cooking vessels. She cleaned up the fridge and went to the supermarket. She helped a great deal. Anubhav worked for two days, cleaning up, giving the curtains for sewing, getting a plumber to repair two leaky taps, arranging the delivery of a cooking gas cylinder . . . that kind of thing.

The flat was too large for me to use so it was decided that two bedrooms would be locked up.

Sharayu Maushi stayed over for two days. She put the curds to set; then she explained the life cycle of milk to me: from milk to curds, from curds to buttermilk, from buttermilk to white butter or ghee. This was, I vaguely realized, a rite of passage. It was something Aai should have done for me. In front of the guests, Aai spoke her mind to me and to Sharayu Maushi. Aseem joined in with some shouting of his own. Baba even begged with folded hands. I could see that it wasn't about me; it was about how close the wedding was.

I haven't seen Tanay. Not when I left the house and not for the two months that I have been living here. Certain things have become clearer but there's only so far you can probe. I've had some trial runs at living alone, but this is real. I still feel the need to be called when I've woken up, still feel the need to ask someone to get me a cup of tea. There's no phone at home. That means I have to plan my trips to the grocer so that I make all my calls and buy whatever I need and then come back upstairs. I don't have my bike which means I can't just up and go wherever I want. I've had to learn the bus routes, study the timetables.

I have to heat the milk myself. And then, how long can you survive on Maggi noodles and eggs, even in various forms? Today, I cooked some potatoes. You get packets of rotis at the grocer. Sometimes I still feel, when I'm returning from the office in the evening, that there should be someone to open the door, to ask me whether I want a hot cuppa. Most other times, it's a blessing. I only sweep and swab on Sunday. Otherwise, I just throw mats about. You know, it's true: vegetables are expensive. But a large cabbage can last me for three days. The fridge is old; after every two days, it has to be allowed to take a breather. I turn it off and then empty the tray which has filled up with water. Yesterday, two cleaning women turned up to inquire if I needed any help. I can't take any more people than is strictly necessary so I turned them away. Anyway, I don't generate enough work to keep a servant occupied. I've told the paper boy to bring me the newspaper. He's in the fifth or sixth standard and quite bright. I'm going to buy him some storybooks to read. I have also discovered that washing a vessel in which milk has been heated is the most trying job in the world. When I bring the trash to the door, the woman who comes to clear it tries to peek past me into the house. I have no idea what she wants. 'Twenty-four hours is not enough time,' my mother would often say. I have now begun to understand what she meant.

But there's one thing I have which no one else does. In the evening, when I have the time, I take a plastic bag with a towel in it, and quietly descend the stairs. I loop around the housing society's lawn and reach the back. There's a swimming pool, full of clean water, glittering in the light of the setting sun. It's beautiful and, in the cool of the evening, few people bother to come.

In my swimsuit, I stand on the side and raise my arms and then leap into that deep-blue water.

Translator's Note

I would like to thank Shanta Gokhale for suggesting *Cobalt Blue* to me. When I read it, I was struck by its simplicity, symmetry and daring. Its basic story is simple: a young man arrives as a paying guest and catalyses the lives of two siblings: a brother and sister.

Kundalkar's telling of it is likewise simple. The first half takes the form of a direct address to the missing young man. This immediately presented a small but telling problem for the translator. Tanay uses 're' constantly. It gives his monologue an intensity, a spontaneity and an affectionate intimacy that has no equal in English. I tried to use the word 'love' as a substitute (as in, 'You would, wouldn't you, love?') but it was not equal in valency or intensity.

Finally, I had to abandon the attempt to find a substitute and accept that there are some things you simply cannot communicate.

The second half takes the shape of a diary that the sister writes. Now we see the same set of events from another position, another perspective. This often makes one's heart ache; surely Anuja and Tanay could have talked? Surely, those years of growing up together in the same house should mean something? But perhaps they don't; perhaps what really matters is the intensity of the time you spend together rather than the length of it.

In many cases, I have chosen to retain some of the original Marathi words. Aai and Baba for instance for mother and father; and the ceremony of the kelvan. In this day and age, anyone who wants to find out what a kelvan is can do so. Fairly reliable information is a couple of clicks away on a website designed specially for such inquiries.

As readers we all know that we should find out the exact meaning of every unknown word we encounter in a book. We know this but we live in an imperfect world and we are imperfect readers. Sometimes, the sheer pace of a narrative will carry us along and there will be no time to check the meaning of the architrave behind which the diamonds have been stashed, just one step ahead of the bad guys. Sometimes, we act on instinct, as so many Indian children did when reading Enid Blyton's descriptions of midnight feasts. Far better to dream up what a scone is, far better to let it explode in a million flavours on your tongue than to look it up and discover its somewhat quotidian doughiness. Most times, we get the sense of the word from the context and read on and through. This is true even when we are not reading books in translation. I have never bothered to stop for an architrave. I don't bother to find a recipe for polenta. I get the general gist and rush on. I expect my readers will do the same when they are guests at Manjiri's kelvan or inhaling the scent of chaafa from the imaginary bedroom Tanay builds or shielding their ears from sutli-bombs on a night of celebration.

As readers we expect narratives to fall into seemly timelines. But neither Tanay nor Anuja respect the sequential. Smitten, broken, rebuilt, they tell their stories as memories spill over, as thoughts surface. They move from the present to the past and back to the present without so much as an asterisk to help you adjust. Tanay says things again and again, as if he wants to reassure himself, as if repetition will fix what has happened in his memory. Once you get used to this, you realize that this is how we grieve, how we remember, in the present tense and in the past, all at once, because the imagined future must now be abandoned.

Finally, this is my first attempt at translation. I would like to thank Neela Bhagwat for her assistance with some of the trickier bits and the sociological implications of some of the phrasings; and Shanta Gokhale (again) for listening to the drafts. Sachin, just your luck that I get to cut my teeth on *Cobalt Blue* but thanks for trusting me with it.

JERRY PINTO
November 2012

About the Author

Sachin Kundalkar is a novelist, playwright, and filmmaker who won a National Film Award for Best Screenplay for the film *Gandha* in 2008. He lives in Mumbai.

About the Translator

Jerry Pinto's debut novel, *Em and the Big Hoom*, won the 2012 Hindu Literary Prize, and his novel *Helen* won a National Film Award for Best Book on Cinema in 2007. He lives in Mumbai.

Publishing in the Public Interest

Thank you for reading this book published by The New Press. The New Press is a nonprofit, public interest publisher. New Press books and authors play a crucial role in sparking conversations about the key political and social issues of our day.

We hope you enjoyed this book and that you will stay in touch with The New Press. Here are a few ways to stay up to date with our books, events, and the issues we cover:

- Sign up at www.thenewpress.com/subscribe to receive updates on New Press authors and issues and to be notified about local events
- Like us on Facebook: www.facebook.com/new pressbooks
- Follow us on Twitter: www.twitter.com/the newpress

Please consider buying New Press books for yourself; for friends and family; or to donate to schools, libraries, community centers, prison libraries, and other organizations involved with the issues our authors write about.

The New Press is a 501(c)(3) nonprofit organization. You can also support our work with a tax-deductible gift by visiting www.thenewpress .com/donate.